In Armageddon 2419 A.D. a twentieth century man arose from the past to save his country. Now he must face

THE RETURN OF THE HAN

"Do you make treaties with mice, with lice? Neither do the Han traffic with humans; we exterminate!"

"You are destroyed," Entallador spat, "here and everywhere, your cities smashed, your armies dust!"

"The Han have risen again. Our robot fleets will now decontaminate Earth. This time there will be no mercy for the despoilers. No single human gene will survive. Tell your North American masters that!" He swept a hand across unseen controls and the vidplate exploded.

JOHN ERIC HOLMES

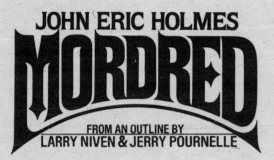

MORDRED

FROM AN OUTLINE BY
LARRY NIVEN & JERRY POURNELLE

ace books
A Division of Charter Communications Inc.
A GROSSET & DUNLAP COMPANY
360 Park Avenue South
New York, New York 10010

MORDRED

An ACE Book
by arrangement with
Thomas Bouregy & Company, Inc.

First Ace printing: January 1980

2 4 6 8 0 9 7 5 3 1
Manufactured in the United States of America

To Lou Mallory

I

Puerto Nateles was burning. A trading center for the sparse population of South America, hours ago the town had been leveled by *dis* rays: only the plaza before the cathedral was relatively clear of smouldering rubble, and here an emergency hospital had been set up. Fortunately, the weather was mild, for there was no shelter for the wounded.

On the screen in the Niagra briefing room the view of the devastated port was replaced by the black mustached face of the local boss. "Han, señores, do not doubt it. I served in the great revolt. I know them. The ship, it came from the north, beamed my city, and then it headed south on its repulsor rays." Remarkably, the South American leader spoke with very little accent.

"Señor Entallador," a staff officer said, "We'll get a rocket with medical supplies on its way to you within the hour. The MexTex Confed can launch it. What worries me is that the attacker

1

could be the advance of some larger force that was somehow overlooked in the War of Liberation."

"I tell you it is Han," the South American said. "Si, we have the local bandits, but those we manage. I remember the Han; that ship was not human. But from where? What does the Generalisimo Rogers think?"

"Rogers is off inspecting the new ship at Badlands Air Base," Major Sally Dupre said.

"We'll ultraphone him immediately," General Gordon assured. "Meanwhile, may we land rockets from the Colorado Union at your base?"

"From already yes!" when excited, Señor Entallador was not strong on Anglish syntax.

"Then we'll get a combat group down there. For the time being they'll be under your command. Beam out."

The group at Niagra Central looked at one another. "After all these years," Dupre mused.

"Entallador ought to know," the general said.

"There's been no contact with a live Han for twenty years."

"Seventeen," someone corrected. "South China Sea, 2462."

"Still seems incredible that a fighting pocket of them could be alive," General Gordon said. "We'd better call Rogers."

"Let the old man sleep."

"He may be old but he's still Commander in Chief. And don't ever say 'old' where he can hear you."

Anthony Rogers, together with a small entourage, was inspecting progress on the *Wilma Deering*. The giant ship lay Gulliver-like in a shallow depression bound to the Earth by crisscrossing bands of ultron. Badlands Air Base was the ad hoc test center for humanity's first true space ship. Inertron, the anti-gravity metal, was still in short supply and the construction was behind schedule. Rogers rather doubted that the ship would be launched in his lifetime.

Nor, though he pretended otherwise, did he really care. Wilma was dead. Why keep reminding him? And why fritter away all these man hours, all these precious materials getting into space when everyone knew the moon and planets were useless—when Earth was so under-populated that most of the land had reverted to forest and the sparkling seas teemed with un-caught fish?

"Equalizing the weight of hull and crew and supplies is not the problem," their guide was saying. "Our only problem has been getting enough inertron."

"The scientific council should keep its priorities straight," Rogers said. "Inertron is needed for the infantry's jump belts and flying harness; also in hulls and rocket motors for the air force."

"Right, sir." seconded Rogers' personal pilot, Lt. Will Holcomb. Like Rogers, he wore a gray-and-blue flyer's uniform, complete with black leather helmet, boots, and rocket pistol at hip. But unlike his pilot, Rogers had taken the liberty of removing his helmet with its self-contained ultraphone. The other thing in which he differed was more significant; unlike his pilot, Rogers wore no insignia of rank.

Their coveralled guide was one of the crew

selected for the *Wilma Deering*'s maiden flight. "There she is, sir. You can get a good view of her from here."

The ship was impressive but no classic beauty. Rogers supposed Wilma would have liked that. The old Han warships had resembled giant dirigibles without the suspended control car, engines, or rudders. The *Wilma Deering* was a huge disc.

It was tethered thirty feet above ground; enough of the inertron hull had been assembled to counterbalance the ship's weight that without anchors she would have been flung from Earth.

"We've decided on liquid fuel for the rockets," the crewman-to-be said as he walked under the ship. "Harris Effect motors use atmospheric gases, but this baby will have to carry her own reaction mass. The *dis* ray motors can convert anything, but water's easiest to handle."

"Easier than whiskey," Rogers mumbled as he tried to ignore his throbbing feet. He had been told that the Han *dis* ray did not really disintegrate matter as everyone had believed during the War, but it dispersed it. The battles at the end of the War of Liberation had been accompanied by clouds of dust and gas—molecules of quondam American troops and equipment.

The resultant energy release was small; if the process had released the energy of the atom, the Han *dis* ray screens around their besieged cities would have released cosmic quantities of heat— and destroyed not only its atmosphere, but Earth itself. Anything within range was instantaneously teleported at molecular, not subnuclear random.

"Where," Rogers asked, "are you going to get water on Mars?" He was tempted to ask why anybody would go there.

"Ice caps. If they're not ice we can use solid CO_2 —or sand, or rock for that matter."

They belted up through an open hatch into the ship. Rogers prided himself on doing that without help. Each new infirmity drove him to greater efforts to retain his strength and agility. He landed upright, steadying himself with his left hand. Habit kept his right hand free to draw a pistol.

"When I went to sleep, scientists thought Mars was probably inhabited. What do you think now?" Rogers referred to his suspended animation in a lost mine in 1927.

Fielding perked up. "There was fairly solid evidence against it in the early days of space flight." He was taking off on his favorite subject. "Of course, after the great cataclysm and the atomic war that preceded the Han invasion all research stopped. The Ancients—" He remembered who he was talking to.

Rogers smiled. "I am ancient in more ways than one."

"Here are the ray batteries, sir."

"About the ancients—?"

"They believed Mars had little atmosphere and the polar caps were carbon dioxide. Of course we can liquefy CO_2 and use it as easily as water."

"I wonder why the Han never tried space flight," Rogers mused, then muttered: "They probably knew better."

A young woman in coveralls looked up as they entered the control cabin. "Hello, Jake. Who are your friends?"

"Peg, meet Marshal Anthony Rogers. And his pilot, Lieutenant Holcomb," he added as an afterthought.

"*Smash*, sir!" She jumped up to pump his hand. "I've always hoped to meet you. What do you think of the *Wilma Deering*?"

"My wife would have loved it," Rogers said diplomatically. "Who are you?"

"Peggy Biskani, electronics tech for the shakedown crew."

"Biskani?"

"Navaho, Marshal, not Chinese. My parents fought in the War of Liberation."

"Miss Biskani, we never fought the Chinese. The Han conquered them first and interbred. They adopted Chinese ways. What the original Han looked like we'll never know—except that they were not human."

A light flashed on the board and the girl answered. "For you, Marshal." She gestured him into the seat.

General Gordon appeard on the screen. "Tony! Bad news: A Han raid in South America!"

Rogers stared. "After all these years . . . where could they have hidden?"

"This gang boss, Entallador, is no fool. He says it was Han."

"Only one ship? Could be a rival gang."

"Would he invite us to land a military presence in his territory just to get the edge on a neighbor? We've sent help."

"Where was it?"

Gordon told them.

"Shall I program a course, sir?" Lt. Holcomb asked.

"Boss Entallador agreed to let us land troops?"

"He begged for them."

"I'm on my way. Tell your combat team to obey him. They remain under his orders; I'll just be an observer."

"Tony, this may be a ruse by the surviving Han to get you."

"After all these years they've probably forgotten who I am. But I thought we'd rooted them all out." Rogers did not know whether his venerable presence would do the Peruvian boss any good—but it would sure as hell do Rogers more good than ceremonial visits to some goddam space ship. "I'll make you a report when I get there, Gordon. Beam out.

"Looks like my inspection will be delayed for a while," he said to the others. "Carry on."

"Oh, Marshal," Peggy Biskani said, "Do be careful. We want you on the *Wilma Deering*'s maiden voyage."

"Ready, Holcomb?" Rogers asked, ignoring the gushing tech.

"Waiting, sir."

They belted to where the *Eagle* rested, nose and tail tied down. Holcomb helped Rogers into the squat, cylindrical ship and closed the ultron canopy. The ground crew cast off and the ship drifted up. Holcomb opened power and the *dis* ray in the nose glowed a faint blue. The ray was tuned to displace only nitrogen, snatching it out of the air in front of them, compressing it in the inertron chamber, letting it jet out the rear. Holcomb gradually upped speed until he was supersonic.

Rogers watched the rolling wilderness of

America glide beneath them. After the Han invasion the population had been reduced to a handful of warring gangs hiding in the forests and swamps which the conquerors disdained. Since the defeat of the Han and the destruction of their cities the scattered population of America had hardly begun to come out of hiding. Small towns, open farmland, and no roads, since transport was by rocket ship. America looked much as it must have to the Indians.

Holcomb kept out of the regular air lanes; he was moving too fast to dodge lumbering cargo rockets. It was night when they set down and Puerto Nateles was still burning.

The ships from MexTex were slower so Rogers and Holcomb were the first reinforcements. The unfortunate locals seemed to think Rogers' presence solved their energy problem.

Entallador, a short, dark man with full black mustache, had been on the go since the attack, but still he insisted on having the Marshal inspect his meager forces. He wore a missile belt with rocket pistols on each hip, but unlike some bosses Rogers had visited Entallador needed no bodyguard.

Rogers left Holcomb in the *Eagle* to confer with the arriving American ships—and ready to take off. If a Han ship showed up the *Eagle* had more chance in the air than sitting.

They visited the field hospital where surgeons operated amid flies, without anaesthetic. Most injuries were from falling buildings or fires but some had lost limbs to *dis* rays. The neat, surgical amputations were unmistakable.

The boss led the way. "Now we go to see my rocket batteries. I do not have much."

He didn't have much: two long guns in trees at the north end of the port, one in the plaza. Entallador had experienced gunners, but only a pitiful dozen rockets. There were rocket pistols among the populace, some flying belts, and plenty of jump belts.

"Your wounded and your headquarters cannot move and you need firepower to protect them," Rogers said as politely as possible. "But you'll want to disperse the rest of your people. Do you have aircraft?"

Their few high speed ships had been dissed. They had some floating airsleds to carry cargo from the fishing fleet and lumber from the jungle.

"How low was the Han when he attacked?"

"Three hundred meters," the boss said. "Then they rose and flew off east toward the mountains. My men try to follow on belts—the ship too fast."

"Run up all the sleds and lifters you can on ultron wire till they're high enough to bother the Han," Rogers suggested. "Anchor them to anything heavy so any low-flying Han will tangle in the wires."

"Corbaz!" The Peruvian turned and began issuing orders. Within an hour he had anti-gravity "barrage balloons" surrounding the port. It wasn't much but at least it might slow the Han a little, give the rocket gunners a chance.

That accomplished, Entallador offered Rogers a bed, but he returned to his ship. Holcomb had volunteered the Eagle as part of the barrage curtain. He let down a line, which Rogers pantingly climbed with the aid of his belt. The Eagle's seats folded into narrow couches; when Holcomb volunteered to keep first watch the old man didn't argue.

Dawn and three American rocket ships came. They landed a medical team, heavy long-gun squads, and a *dis* ray weapons group. The commanding officer of the airships threw a salute as Rogers entered the bank building Entallador had commandeered for headquarters. "Good morning, Marshal," he said. "I'm Major Lewis. What's our sit?"

Rogers returned his salute. "Entallador's the boss here, Major. I'm just an observer."

The Peruvian began a polite protest but Rogers waved him down. "No, señor, I'm too old. Lieutenant Holcomb, myself, and our ship are available to you for scout duty."

The Americans had led the rebellion against the Han. As a result, America dominated the political and military machinery of the world. Deference to the American military came naturally to Entallador, who was a realist, and deference to the legendary leader of the Americans came naturally to Major Lewis. Rogers had trouble getting them to believe he would not take charge. He wondered what they would have made of Wilma.

Entallador and Major Lewis had another problem. They had no idea where the enemy had come from. Han ships "walked" on repulsor rays and were not as fast as American rockets, but the raider was long gone and could be up to any mischief. The old Han ships had tapped broadcast power. Lewis's detectors picked up no flicker of emission.

Entallador sent flying scouts into the jungle. One man reported large patches of jungle northeast through the Andes were cut or crushed, which probably meant Han rep propulsion had smashed them. Major Lewis dispatched two ships to investigate.

Upcoast a patrol leader reported a cigarshaped object on the beach, but when she had led her patrol closer it disappeared into the water. This intrigued Rogers. He told Entallador that he and Holcomb would take the *Eagle* to look the area over. The Boss ultraphoned his scouts to expect them.

"Take care, Marshal," Major Lewis said. "I'm keeping one ship in reserve. We'll come if you call us."

The desert ended abruptly at the edge of the ocean. Holcomb spotted the scouts, circled the *Eagle*, came down within a few feet of the ground as Rogers slid back the canopy and jumped. Even with a belt reducing the aged hero's weight to grams, Rogers' bones felt the jolt of landing.

The patrol consisted of two women and a man. They had machetes, rocket pistols, and a single ultraphone. All wore green camouflage gear, which was not that useful in the desert. None understood Anglish, nor did Rogers have more than a word or two of twenty-fifth century Español. With gestures they reiterated that something *muy grande* had been spotted on the shoreline below, and that they had gone to investigate. They had first seen it from a cliff several hundred feet from the surf. Rogers could see no sign of a ship having landed, nor any track suggesting rep rays.

A woman gestured out to sea. The thing, she

pantomimed, had flown out over the waves and vanished. She had marked the spot, called in a report, and sat down to wait. Rogers pointed to his watch. Two hours, she indicated with two fingers. They had only jump belts, no way to continue the chase over water.

Rogers flipped on his helmet phone. "Holcomb, they think it went into the water. I'm going to fly out and look. Follow me, but keep high. Try the ultrascope on the sea bottom."

"Don't you think you ought to return to the ship, sir? That thing may still be out there."

Rogers grunted. He belted over birds feeding on the Humboldt Current's inexhaustible anchovies. At my age I'm expendable, he thought. What better way to go than fighting my old enemies? And yet he knew he was talking rubbish. He might be old but he was still not grown up enough to hand over the mantle of leadership as gracefully as old Boss Ciardi had passed it on to him when Rogers and the war were young.

He knew he was a figurehead and no longer a leader. To his staff he was probably a doddering old fool. Why was he risking the lives of his pilot or the Peruvians with this gesture?

For a while he saw only whitecaps and feeding gulls. Behind him Holcomb climbed to a thousand meters and beamed the scope. There was silence, then Holcomb's voice came: "Something moving on the bottom. Could be a whale. Nope, a ship!"

"Where?" Rogers cut rockets and drifted just over the waves.

"Ahead, left about fifteen degrees. Get back to the ship, Marshal, here it comes!"

The snout of the armored ship broke the surface like some prehistoric beast. Water churned as the big dirigible-like craft flung itself into the air on repulsor rays. A hatch in the forward hull snapped open. Rogers belted off. Pale blue *dis* flared behind him. He heard the clap as it died and air rushed to fill the vacuum.

Rogers guided his flight by shifting his weight, using the inertron belt as unthinkingly as he wore his shoes. He saw *dis* flash again, sweep the cliff top from which he had flown. The Peruvians jumped, but not in time. Two of them vanished.

The Han ship was gathering speed now, stalking above the water on two sets of repulsors. "Flit south, Marshal!" Holcomb was high above the enemy. He rolled and dived. Missiles flashed from the ship's stubby wings. Rogers belted, gaining altitude as he drew his pistol. He selected his heaviest round of longrange ammunition and forlornly fired his rocket pistol at a hundred-meter Han ship.

One of Holcomb's rockets exploded against the armored hull. The other armor-piercing round missed and did not explode when it hit the ocean below. The Han kept moving. The *Eagle* flashed past and zoomed up over the sere cliff tops. The *dis* ray snapped after him. The beam caught him as he turned but the inertron shielding held. As Rogers swooped up and over the enemy Holcomb turned and came in again.

The Han ship was gaining velocity. The *Eagle* fired two more rockets at close range. Both hit and the metal cigar rocked. Holcomb was over the ocean and circling for his next attack before the Han could respond. A ray battery in the stern

popped open. Pale rays dissed the air beside the
American, trying to create vacuum and force the
ship into a turn. Rogers could see that the dis
gunners were experienced or well trained.

Dissing air pockets had worked against inertron
armored floaters, tumbling them frequently. But
Holcomb was moving too fast; he flew through. If
the rays ever held him, though, he would be in
trouble, for his jets drew nitrogen from the air.
If the Han could envelop the little ship in a
vacuum . . .

In the old days Rogers had knocked the rep ray
stilts from under Han ships by rocketing explosives into them. Later the Han had learned to
shield their rep ray with dis. Now he flew parallel
to the enemy and aimed at the slanting rep rays
that drove her. He gripped the gun in both
hands—he was not as good a shot as he used to
be—and fired. The explosion rocked the Han
ship.

"Get out of there, Tony!" Holcomb screamed.
Disrespectful address to a senior, Rogers thought.
He laughed. Blood pounded in his ears. By ginger,
I am still alive, he thought. There was a crash as
dis flipped toward him. He had forgotten that he
wore no inertron armor. If the ray hit he would
"go to zero", as Wilma had taught him to say.
Nothing would remain but the indestructible flying belt and that a scientist had once told him
would probably end up bobbing in one of the
Earth-Sun trojan points.

Holcomb was on the far side of the ship and two
rays were trying to keep him pinned in vacuo. His
jets stuttered. An American rocket slammed the
stern of the bigger ship and threw the gunners off

target. Rogers, suddenly realizing that he too was in this game, dived below the cliff out of the line of fire. Dis sheared the edge of the cliff. Rocks and sand rained, striking his helmet and belt. Holcomb rocketed past his enemy once again, curved up and struggled to turn.

Rogers eased his way up the cliff face. There were nests in the rock and as he passed by the mother gulls lunged, beaks agape and wings flapping.

"Where are you, Marshal?" Holcomb's voice was calmer now. "All right. I see you. Stay there and I'll pick you up."

"I'll survive. Keep after him!"

"I've fired half my missiles and haven't even scratched his wax job."

"This time come in on his portside," Rogers directed. The enemy ship was still headed for the mountains but it had slowed. Maybe it was coming back. The Eagle shrieked by him again, swiftly re-engaged the lumbering behemoth. Dis rays caught the rocket but did not hold. While the gunners were concentrating on Holcomb, Rogers belted, keeping low.

"Into my turn, Marshal," Holcomb called.

"Good. I'm going to hit both starboard repulsors. If he starts to tip, hit him portside with all you've got!"

The black dot of the rocket began to grow and Rogers carefully pumped every shell he had into the Han repulsors. Explosions staggered the Han vessel and it started to roll.

"Let him have it!"

Rockets exploded against the ship's armor on the side away from Rogers. Dis hissed and slammed. Huge tracts of sand disappeared as the Han vessel heeled.

"He's not rolling enough!" Holcomb cried. "I'm going to sideswipe him!"

"Watch—" Rogers started to yell—dis rays took the ground from beneath him. He fell gently because of his flying belt, but flowing sand caught him and pulled him down. He cried out and Holcomb heard. The next thing Rogers heard was not intended for him.

"They got the old man!" Holcomb gasped. "You bastards!" The *Eagle* slammed into the Han cruiser, ricochetted into a hillside, losing a wing in the process.

But Holcomb's suicidal ramming had rolled the Han ship enough so that the repulsors no longer pointed down. The ship was only a few thousand feet up but the Han craft had no inertron plating. Six thousand tons plowed into the earth.

"Holcomb?" Rogers called. He struggled to dig himself out of the sand.

"Marshal? That you?"

"Call me Tony." Rogers blasted free of the sand and belted off toward the Han wreck.

II

———◆—◆—◆———

The *Eagle* was smashed but she could be made to fly again. Lt. Holcomb had a broken arm, a cut over one eye, and would also fly again. Rogers splinted Holcomb's arm, improvised a sling, patched the eye, medicated his patient, and then rested while he kept watch on the Han ship. His heart was beating irregularly and he was short of breath. Gunning down enemy ships is really not for eighty-year olds. Still, he grinned; he hadn't felt so good since Wilma had finally died. *Now what made me think that?*

They called headquarters. Back came an urgent request to look for the Peruvians. Rogers had forgotten them. He was certain he'd seen a couple of them disintegrated, but how about the third? Holcomb volunteered, but Rogers vetoed that idea; the pilot was in no shape to go belting about. They opened a tin of emergency rations and Rogers had a bite and some coffee before he took off. In spite of the food he was feeling each of his eighty three years. He circled the wreck of the Han ship. No movement. He had hoped for a prisoner. He

17

needed information. Slowly cruising the coastline, he found no trace of the scouting party. He called his own ship periodically and finally Holcomb responded.

"Señor Entallador is sending reinforcements by belt . . . Tony. He asked about the scouts."

"He's a good commander then. But I've no good news."

"One of them was his daughter-in-law."

"Blast! Tell him I'm doing my best. How are you?"

"The shot you gave me is starting to work."

"Good. If the ultrascope's working, get it onto the Han ship. I don't want those wicked little wasters coming after me."

"Right sir, and good hunting."

The sun was going down and an onshore wind was rising. When he found the woman she was unconscious, hanging inert from her jump belt halfway down the cliff. The wind was slamming her against the rocks. He cursed.

"I've found one woman," he ultraphoned so that Holcomb could call back to headquarters. He swooped down and took the straps of the wounded scout's belt in his left hand. Her arms and face were badly bruised, but she was breathing.

Flying low and trying to keep the smashed *Eagle* between himself and the enemy ship, Rogers delivered his burden to Holcomb and they laid her out on the sand.

Holcomb knelt. "Can't be more than eighteen."

"Get her clothes off and see if she's hurt anywhere else. Did you report to Puerto Nateles? How's the ultrascope?"

"The boss there hopes this is his daughter-in-law. He's on his way with reinforcements. The scope's working but something keeps me from seeing inside the Han ship—*take her clothes off!?*" Even by Roger's standards twenty fifth century America was somewhat prudish.

"What'll he say if she's hit and we let her bleed to death? Where's the med kit?"

"In your compartment. I'm not sure I like this, Tony."

"You're so embarrassed you want her to die? Follow your orders. Now let's see what I get on the scope." But he was unable to probe more than the outer armor. The inside of the Han ship was opaque to the spy ray. He tried to beam through a dis ray port. "Not seeing a damn thing!" he complained. "How are you doing?"

Holcomb made a strange noise. "She seems, ah, intact. But I can't get her uniform back on with one hand. Throw me down a blanket or something before shock hits her."

Hiding a grin Rogers did so. Then they folded a cockpit seat down into a cot and painfully hoisted the girl into the *Eagle*. She was still unconscious, but groaning a little. Rogers considered administering a syrelle of morphine, but he was afraid of the terrible things this dangerous drug could do to the unsuspecting. Anyhow, help was on the way.

The sun threw long shadows of the downed rocket over ray tracks in the desert before the Peruvians arrived. Rogers was eager to break into the Han ship but his force consisted of a tired old man, a wounded pilot, and a delirious girl. He waited.

Entallador arrived with household troops, three

scouts, and a medtech; some wild-goose chase
had drawn off the last of Major Lewis's ships but
the tough little Peruvian boss had not waited. He
was rewarded: the girl was who he had hoped she
would be.

The med saw to the girl and set Holcomb's arm.
Entallador worried over his daughter-in-law but,
though the medtech, whom he called a *mata-
sanos*, wanted to move both patients back to
Puerto Nateles, the boss agreed with Rogers that
they should break into the Han ship at once. Rogers left Holcomb with the girl.

There was only starlight as they surrounded the
downed Han. They showed no light even though
anyone alive inside would probably have detectors. As he struggled to move noiselessly in the
dark Rogers knew that his few remaining days
were just as precious as any young man's lifetime.
Anyone who thought differently was either
young, self deluded, or both. Or was it the danger
itself that made his life so precious to him? Rogers
grinned at his wool-gathering.

Inside the hull he heard clanks and creaks but
nothing happened. Cooling off, he supposed.

A Peruvian found a half-buried hatch. It would
not open. Entallador's dis ray team set up their
weapon and blasted it but it was shielded. Finally
they blew it open with rocket shells. Rogers wondered why they had bothered sneaking up.

The blasted hatch revealed more darkness.
They probed with an electric torch, saw nothing
but bent hull plates and broken instruments. Entallador sent a team—a man and woman—inside.
As the rest waited in silent darkness there came a
sudden "¡*Cuidado!*," then an explosion.

Entallador and two of his men rushed forward, followed by the rest of the party. Rogers waved the rest back down, then followed. The scouts were on the control room deck. The space was littered with glass from instruments and screens, but two screens were still alight. One showed the desert outside, the other was blank. Fastened to the deck in front of the control panel was a padded chair and in it a square metal box was set. Rods, tubes, coax cables projected from the front of this device to the controls. Two longer cables snaked out of the room. Smoke issued from a hole behind the box.

One of the Peruvians moved. Rogers had thought them dead.

"¿Qué pasó?" Entallador demanded of the reviving scout, and learned that he had touched the metal device in the chair and it had moved. When he cried out the girl had shot it: in the tiny space her rocket pistol had stunned them. The girl was reviving now too.

Cables ran from the thing to the ship's ray guns; there was no human or Han on board. After they had searched the wreck twice from end to end, Rogers went out into the starlit night and, free of inertron shielding, used his helmet phone to call Holcomb. He learned that the girl they had rescued was now conscious, and Holcomb relayed a report from Rogers to Major Lewis, whose ships still searched the jungles to the east for sign of Han. Lewis got a fix on them and sent a rocket, hoping to salvage both ships.

Suddenly a greenclad Peruvian bounced from the hatch and caught Rogers by the arm. He spoke urgently in Español and pointed back into the ship. Comprehending only that he was wanted within, Rogers followed him.

The viewscreen had come to life. The face was almost human: pale yellow skin, dark brows, and a faint mustache. Eyes large and dark, obscured by a slight hint of epicanthic fold. He wore a yellow robe and on his hairless head perched a skull cap.

The apparition was clearly struggling to adjust the video from the way he peered into the screen; at a few points on the smashed control panel lights flickered and died. Finally they faintly heard a voice. Rogers recognized the intonation as Han from his long imprisonment during the great war.

He could not understand but it was obvious that the man was questioning who or whatever he thought was in the control room. "Wish I could get a fix on that beam," Rogers muttered. "Holcomb, can you hear me?" But the inside of the enemy ship was shielded from any except Han broadcasts.

The face frowned and gave up. Rogers tried to get a scout to run outside and tell Holcomb to radio Major Lewis that they were in contact, if not communication with the enemy. He got the impression that the scout wished he would speak Español like an intelligent person. Suddenly a new face filled the screen.

This was a face with eyes that looked through people instead of at them. Black robe with a red and yellow device. He was hairless, with the unstudied arrogance of a shark. Breaking off a conversation with someone out of sight, he moved closer to the transmitter until his face filled the screen.

Suddenly his voice boomed into the ship. Clearly angry, he snapped orders at someone out of view. The screen dimmed, brightened. More lights came on in the cabin where Rogers and the Peruvians watched.

The Han's eyes widened. "*¿Quienes son?*" he demanded, then repeated it in Anglish, "Who are you? What do you inside a ship of the Heaven Born?"

"*Somos el gobierno legítimo humano,*" Entallador said, "And what do you, sending your murdering ship to slaughter women and children?"

The Han reverted to Español. "What do we do? Have you no eyes? We exterminate. Do you make treaties with mice, with lice? Neither do the Han traffic with humans!"

"You are destroyed," the Peruvian spat, "here and everywhere, your cities smashed, your armies dust!"

"The Han have risen again. Our robot fleets will now decontaminate Earth. This time there will be no mercy for the despoilers. No single human gene will survive. Tell your North American masters that!" He swept a hand across unseen controls and the vidplate exploded. As the Peruvians dodged the shower of shattered glass there was a crackle in the control panel. Metal began to flow lavalike down the side of the cabin.

"Out of the ship!" Rogers cried, "She's going to blow!" After some confusion over precedence at the hatch—everyone thought someone else should leave first—they all belted it to safety.

Actually, the ship did not explode, though heat waves emanating from it gave the stars an extra twinkle. They felt it even a mile away where they had stopped. Within minutes the ship was glowing. Then, like a deflating balloon, it collapsed and the glow became too bright to look at.

"I wonder if the Señor Han thinks he got us," Entallador said.

"Maybe—I hope so—What exactly did he have to say in there?"

The Peruvian boss told Rogers what had been said.

In the morning, when the Han ship had cooled, they inspected it again, but there was nothing they could learn from the wreckage.

Rogers kicked the fused mass of the Han raider. He had never seen a robot ship, nor a Han screened from ultrascope. How much had the Han learned from the War of Liberation? How many were there? Where? Where would they strike next?

At least they must be short of fighters; the makeshift robot pilot had been sitting in a seat designed for a human body! Short on men, short on critical supplies, but equipped with *new technology*. This ship had been shielded and had not run on broadcast power.

Rogers felt the old excitement. His knowledge of artillery, gained in World War One, plus a very real military genius for the incredible technology of the new America, had carried him to leadership and to victory. But now the Han were back, seemingly more deadly than ever.

"Señor Entallador," he said, "There's nothing to learn here. As soon as Lewis sends a ship we rocket out of here."

Major Lewis was glad to see them back but Rogers sensed his disappointment at the loss of the Han ship, felt a slight sense of guilt. In the old days Rogers had never looked back: now he ran endless mental replays, wondering how else he might have handled it.

"We think we've located another base back in the jungle," Lewis said, oblivious to his superior's internal conflicts, "but we'll check out the ocean bottom where you ran into the bandit."

Rogers hardly heard him, he was so tired, but before seeking out his tent he hobbled across the plaza to the med center; he felt much too fragile for the jolts of belting. An American medtech took time from her wounded patients to check his heart. "Not good, Marshal," she said as she scanned the printout. "But I don't suppose anybody could make you rest."

"Don't see how I can right now."

"Let me give you this anyway." She took an ampule from one of the scattered crates and injected its contents into his arm. "These too." She gave him a vial of cardiotropin tablets. "Come back in a couple of days."

"Thanks," he said, and wondered if he'd be alive to keep the appointment.

Out in the plaza again, he ran into Holcomb, whose arm was in a fresh sling. "I know the way to our quarters," the pilot volunteered.

"How's Entallador's daughter?"

"Yolanda's doing fine. Her husband was killed in the raid."

"I'd wondered about that," Rogers said. "Any chance of putting the *Eagle* back together?"

"No parts or electronics. And the military can't spare any techs. It'll take a tow back to MexTex."

"How did you find out about Entallador's son?"

"I asked—some of the HQ personnel speak Anglish."

Rogers grinned. "Idle curiosity, I suppose."

The young man seemed surprised. "I wondered why he didn't show up when we landed."

When they reached their tent it was still daylight and the camp was abuzz with the rumor that some sort of Han installation had been discovered in the mountains. The run-in with the robot warship was already old news.

"I'm going to rest," Rogers said. "Scout if you want." He lay on the cot aching, pondering the cosmic injustice that blessed the young with sleep when it was the old who needed it. But finally Rogers did sleep.

Next day he felt better. He persuaded Entallador to let him accompany a team of scouts into an area of the mountains where there were two cleared sites, about thirty miles apart, which could be Han landing fields. Ultrascopy from American rockets had revealed nothing at one site for as deep as the rays could penetrate—but a large area impenetrable to the probe had been found just underground at the second. Surveillance was being maintained, with one of Lewis's ships hovering over the more likely site. The boss introduced Rogers to the Peruvians he was to accompany.

Foso was short, almost a dwarf, with muscular legs and torso and a bulging forehead. Though grotesque, he was cheerful and his two woman assistants seemed to find nothing odd in his appearance. Sexual equality had bothered Rogers when he had first awakened from the world of 1927—until he had seen the North American amazons in action. Now he would trust a squad of

women like his dear departed wife, Wilma, more
than the toughest doughboys from his first war.

Foso and his women wore the green camouflage humans had used in the War of Liberation.
They had rocket pistols, machetes, and one of the
still scarce and valuable ultraphones. An anti-
gravity sled had been stacked with supplies and
followed on a rope, like a captive balloon.

The Peruvians had only jump belts. They went
into the jungle in long low leaps, avoiding the
overhanging trees, last one towing the sled. Each
half hour they changed places.

Rogers used just enough jet to keep up. His belt
required no muscular exertion, save for twisting
his body to turn or lift. After so many years flying
was second nature. But his companions had to
work at their jumps despite their belts that reduced weight to a few grams, so they tired before
he did. When they stopped to rest Foso would
answer Rogers' questions as best he could. His
Anglish grammar was scant but his hands were
eloquent.

For hours they travelled along what had once
been a wide highway but was now little different
from the rest of the jungle. This country, Foso
assured him, had once been populated. Even before the coming of the Han something had wiped
out most of South America. This, Foso said, was
el marro del Señor, which Rogers supposed was
the same "Lucifer's Hammer" of North America.
Years later the Han conquest had driven the few
survivors into hiding. Jungle, puna, and pampa
had revived while the Han slowly degenerated in
their fortified cities.

Then the War of Liberation had changed humanity from nuisance to doom. The development of inertron weapons had enabled the North American gangs to fight back, and in this struggle Anthony Rogers' other-century, massed army viewpoint had brought him to prominence. The revolt had spread round the world, ended in utter and complete victory. Everyone had thought the Han were annihilated.

Foso pointed out ruins which present-day Peruvians mined for their metals. Rogers remembered that the South America of his five hundred year old day had also contained lost cities of mysterious origin, covered by luxuriant growth. He tried to express some of this to Foso.

"Quechua." The dwarf said it proudly.

"What's that?"

"Old Indians. King called Inca. We Quechua. Talk on radio. Han only talk Español. You want see old city?"

Rogers wondered what Major Lewis would think if they turned this scout into a rubberneck tour.

They emerged from jungle onto a narrower trail up into the mountains. When the trail switchbacked one scout would jump to the next level and drop a rope, bringing the antigrav sled up. After an afternoon pause for food and rest, the scouts added a few rocks to compensate for the weight of provisions consumed.

Even with his flying belt Rogers began to feel the thin mountain air. Foso bounced up beside him and urged that they go around the mountain to the far side to view his Inca ruins. Then he saw how the old man was wheezing.

"Aaaahh, *soroche*. Man from coast always sick here." He showed Rogers how to take a deep breath, hold it while squeezing down; it was the only way to extract oxygen from the outer space of fourteen thousand feet—unless a man be born with *Quechua* lungs.

After several minutes of grunt-breathing Rogers was rewarded with a disappearance of the clouds of "gnats" which had danced before his eyes. "Yes," he said. "Now what did we come up here for?"

Foso grinned. "White man here put notes in pocket. Never remember take out again."

Rogers wondered why he had not brought oxygen. He had known the Andes were high. While the two women horsed the sled up the mountain and through a narrow pass they took a side trail. Or rather, Foso took the centimeters-wide trail and Rogers flew beside him. Behind them the jungle spread, thinning as it met the coastal desert. There was no sign of habitation.

Rogers studied his map and saw the Han suspect spots were still on the other side of the mountains. The ruins, Foso explained, were on the northeast face of this mountain. When Rogers finally saw them the remnants of stone wall clinging to the cliff were unimpressive. He reminded himself that these stones had been hewed and set by primitives, without flight, without antigravity or power of any kind. These five ton stones had been brought up the mountain by human hands who had not even oxen or mules to help. He wondered if this could be the fabled Macchu Picchu that Hiram Bingham had discovered back in 1911 when Rogers had been a kid admiring the Wright Brothers and Glenn Curtis with their kitelike aeroplanes.

They sat on the squared off boulders Foso's ancestors had used to build their stronghold and gazed down. They were high now but Puerto Nateles and the coast were still invisible.

"Guerra de Liberación," Foso said. "Guards spy here *los aeronaves de Han*." He pointed to ruins above them, then jumped.

"*¡Caramba!*" the dwarf cried "*¡Pronto, mi general, mire!*"

Rogers had learned that *caramba* is the clicking of billiard balls, an interjection much beloved of pious maiden ladies. But he had also learned that Foso was complying with a *manda* not to use strong language, hoping with this vow to gain some concession from a silent god. He jetted up to see what had caused the excitement.

There was a round hole in the rock: a circular tunnel with smooth glazed edges led into the mountain.

"*Dis ray*," Rogers said. "Call the others."

Foso spoke into his helmet phone. Rogers could not understand but he sensed that these hissing tonalities were not Español. The dwarf turned to Rogers. "Come fast or bring all?"

"Where's the longrange ultraphone?"

"Sled."

"Ask one of them to bring it up and the other to stay below with the supplies."

Foso spoke again. Rogers poked around the ancient ruins and the new tunnel, periodically reminding himself to breathe. The dwarf found several discarded food cans.

"From around here?" Rogers asked.

Foso pointed to an ideograph stamped in the metal. It was Han. When the scout arrived with the ultraphone they reported in again. Foso verified their position as Cerro del Huanco above Gemelo Pass.

"We're going in," Rogers said. "Send another troop to reinforce and pick up the supply sled."

"But my orders—" Foso shrugged. Rogers, after all, was the bossissimo. They drew rocket pistols and began the descent into the hole. Rogers helmet light lit a hundred meters of tunnel while they floated straight down. At the bottom the tunnel ended in a great bronze door set into the rock. As Rogers' light hit the door other lights lit up the tunnel. Rogers gripped his pistol and hoped he would not have to use it and probably bring the tunnel down around them.

Seemingly of its own volition the door at the end of the tunnel began to open inward; framed within it was a slim figure that looked perfectly human. Rogers knew from her attire that she was Han: long black hair framed a delicate face with huge sensuous eyes and budlike mouth. One hand was on the door control, the other behind her into a hidden chamber. Her snugfitting scarlet gown was slit to reveal her navel, thin straps concealing her breasts. Her full length skirt was also slit, baring her thigh and a bit more. There was an evocative familiarity in the way she turned her head, eyes widened. Rogers was suddenly wracked by emotions he had thought dead since long before Wilma killed—he meant died. "Ngo-Lan!" he cried, a lament for lost youth.

III

———◆◆◆◆◆———

Ngo-Lan, most seductive, alluring—not woman. Wilma had always insisted they were *females*. But if she lived Ngo-Lan was an old woman, nearly as ancient as Rogers. Yet there was something in this young—female's—oriental beauty, the turn of her head, the silken luxury of her bared thigh that brought Ngo-Lan back to him as vividly as that day she had helped him escape the Han capital—and he had deceived her, left her bound and gagged and gone scuttling back to Wilma.

In his official biography, ARMAGEDDON 2419, Rogers had hardly dared hint at his liaison with the Emperor's favorite.—The Liberator, Father of America did not fornicate with nonhumans. But this couldn't be the same wom—female. That was all too many years ago, another time, another country. The loveliest of the Han was surely dead. Dead as Wilma. Dead as Rogers.

The girl stared at old man and dwarf.

"Ngo-Lan!" Rogers' pistol wavered.

Her eyes widened and she flung herself backward.

The bronze door closed with the smooth click of a treasury vault.

"Wait!" He sprang for the door. . . . there was no handle.

"*Marsical*," Foso began, "what—"

There was a faint hissing. "Don't breathe!" Rogers said.

"*¿Cómo?* You know beautiful person?" Foso began to inquire incredulously when suddenly his face contorted and he began to slump.

Rogers grabbed Foso and sprang for the tunnel mouth.

The dwarf had no pulse when they got to the open. Rogers didn't know whether the gas would only fill the tunnel or if it would come billowing out after him. He beckoned the ultraphonist to follow and belted off upwind, gliding down the face of the cliff several hundred feet into thicker air. Halfway down he met the other woman dragging the sled up. He handed Foso to her and pointed back the way she had come. She stared, then turned. Rogers filled his lungs and jetted back up toward the Han tunnel.

The longrange ultraphone was with the group below. The only trilingual member of the party who knew Anglish was out of action. To go into the tunnel alone was insane even if he could cobble up breathing gear. He grinned. He knew as much about Han cities as anyone alive. Despite his age, this was something he could do better than any young soldier. And there was the girl . . . . How could a man his age go into such a tizzy at the mere sight of a beautiful wom—

female! *Yes Wilma, dear heart, damn it, I'm com-ing!*

Three figures in armor and flying belts came rocketing out of the tunnel. Helmets and air tanks protected them from the gas. They carried dis pistols.

Rogers dived as the Han fired. He was slow but the ancient rock wall came between them. In a moment the rocks were gone but the handheld dis rays were limited; they could burn through stones, but took seconds to do it.

Using hands as wings, he turned a shallow dive into a long arc, belted at full power, and came back up into sight at the far end of the ruined wall. He hoped most devoutly that he would be fast enough. He drew his pistol and snapped off three rounds. A rocket pistol makes almost no noise as the rocket leaves the tube and, unlike a bullet, continues to accelerate.

Dis beams swept up as Rogers belted away from the side of the cliff. The rays missed but his rockets did not. The Han ray shielding was ineffectual against a missile with the punch of an old fashioned artillery shell. One Han blew up. A second jetted clear and continued down the mountainside, straight toward the waiting Peruvians. Exploding shells echoed through the mountains. The third Han was victim to a near miss as one of Rogers' rockets hit bushes twenty meters behind him, tossing rock and dirt. As the enemy soldier flipped in mid-air he dropped his weapon.

"Got you!" Rogers soared wide. He holstered the pistol. No more Han appeared. Downslope, the second Han had been killed by the Peruvians.

The third drifted gently downward, arms dangling.

Rogers slowed before grabbing him and belting down the mountainside. In the old days he would have hit him full tilt in a manner that the referees of an ancient game had called "clipping." But now Rogers had more respect for his ancient bones.

Thoughtlessly he left his prisoner for the Peruvian women to disarm or dissect while he ultraphoned HQ. Major Lewis was astounded. "You're sure it's Han, Marshal? You couldn't be mistaken?"

"Not when I've been nearly zeroed by three of them with *dis!*" Rogers snarled. "Get me some reinforcements. I've taken twenty five per cent casualties."

When Rogers returned to the group he found that Foso had awakened; the gas must have been anaesthetic and not lethal.

With some difficulty Foso had persuaded the women not to dismember the Han with machetes because he knew that Rogers had some unfathomable reason for wanting him alive—but as far as the women were concerned, the no-prisoners tradition of the War of Liberation still prevailed. In those bloodthirsty days Han of all ages and sexes were routinely slaughtered. After suffering centuries of casual genocide the Americans had adopted the Han policy for their own, and persuaded their allies to adopt it as well.

The Han was bound hand and foot. He had dropped his disintegrator and had no other weapon. Rogers looked up at the mountain top. There was no further movement, but as much as he wanted to find the girl, he could not fly unprotected into a gasfilled tunnel guarded by troops armed with dis weapons. He was lucky to have survived—suddenly reaction left him weak and querulous with a return of his chest pain. He took one of his pills.

Foso thought their best bet was to disperse on both sides of the trail, where they could monitor the descent from the Incan ruins. If the Han came at them they could snipe with rockets. If the enemy came from some other direction business would turn bad.

Rogers dispersed the Peruvians as far apart as possible, this being their best defense against sweeping dis. He left the prisoner with Foso and the supply sled unprotected since any Han would surely sweep so obvious a target. They tuned helmet radio and Rogers took up station in a tree. They waited. Once the humans were motionless jungle life took up its noisy routine. Birds, monkeys, insects, but no hint of Han. An hour passed.

When the rocket ship finally settled toward them Rogers' nerves were taut. "Where've you been?" he demanded. "Couldn't find us? It's only the tallest peak in a hundred miles." As he said it he knew he was being childish.

"Approaching with caution, sir," a voice said in his phones. "We're still trying to scope your tunnel. That mountain is remarkably dense."

"They've got it shielded."

"Right, sir. I'm sending a flying squad in to check it out. Signal your position and I'll take you aboard."

As the rocket hovered Rogers projected himself up through an open hatch. A redhaired officer in

Air Force gray was waiting. "Permission to board, captain," Rogers said.

"Honored to have you, Marshal. But—that prisoner—is it necessary for him to live, sir?"

"Stop thinking with your glands, captain. I want him interrogated. Do you have an interpreter aboard? No? I thought not." For a brief moment there stood before the ship commander the Man from the past who had led the Americans in world conquest.

The Peruvians sent the bound Han up on an unballasted belt and a rope, tethered like a balloon. Rogers and the ship commander pulled him through the hatch. They dragged the silent, wide eyed prisoner inside, unsnapped the belt, and slammed him against the bulkhead. The captain motioned. An airman drew a rocket pistol and covered the crouching Han.

"I want my Peruvian team aboard," Rogers said. "One's wounded and they have no armor against a *dis* attack.

"We'll drop them a line. What do we do with this thing?" The captain gestured toward the Han.

"Where's communications?"

"Starboard, sir," the officer answered, staring at the small yellowish shaven headed man. "Is this really a Han, sir? He doesn't look dangerous."

"They conquered us once," Rogers said. He got the prisoner into the crowded com room. Vid plates dominated the main bulkhead. Others were covered with controls and smaller screens. Rogers coerced a reluctant cooperation from the man on duty. They tied the Han into the communicator's seat, facing a large plate. The crewman squeezed in beside Rogers, leaned over the captive and adjusted the ultrawave receiver. When they raised Niagra the duty officer there had to call Intelligence and they had to wake up an interpreter.

The ship commander appeared on a different screen. "My men report the tunnel slagged. We'll have to use the ship's dis ray to open it,"

"Very good, captain. I'll contact you as soon as I've siphoned this prisoner dry." He had to brace himself as the ship flipped and angled in at the mountain top.

Meanwhile at Niagra word had spread that Rogers had a prisoner, and General staffers were crowded into the con room when the interpreter arrived.

The captive betrayed an instant of surprise at hearing his own language, then the sullen mask fell over his face again. The interpreter tried repeatedly while the ship wheeled and tipped under captors and captive.

"Marshal Rogers, I'm afraid it's hopeless," the interpreter was saying when the Han looked up and snapped a brief question. The interpreter answered and then the prisoner was talking, mostly in Rogers' direction and with animation.

"Well, sir," the interpreter said, "I'm not sure how to translate what he called you."

"Thank you." Rogers managed to contain his amusement.

"Mainly, it's that Marshall Anthony Rogers is the defiler of Han culture, a blight on the planet, a plague across the face of the Heaven Born empire, and the enemy of all that is ordained and holy."

"Thanks," Rogers said drily.

"There's more, sir. You have been singled out for personal revenge by Prince Mordred and all lesser beings have been instructed not to kill you."

"Prince *who?*" Faint alarums were stirring in Rogers' subconscious.

The interpreter relayed his question. The prisoner looked at Rogers for a silent moment, then around the cabin.

"Tell him he will be humanely treated if he cooperates."

The Han replied at length to this.

"He will die bravely as befits the Han," the interpreter said. "His name is Lon-Wo. The Han do not stoop to the animality of serial numbers."

"Lon-Wo," Rogers said in Anglish, "What is this base in the mountains used for? We're burning in with *dis*. You may as well save us ten minutes."

"Tunnel open, Marshal," the captain's voice interrupted.

"Be right there. Well?" The prisoner spoke and Rogers waited.

"He says it makes no difference. It was an observation post and by now all personnel will have escaped. He knew they would seal the entrance. He volunteered for a delaying mission. He dies happy."

Rogers felt a moment of confusion. How could a Han have noble motives? "Keep him talking," he snapped, "I'm going to belt out to the tunnel." (But the next time Rogers remembered to ask about the Han, ship personnel were evasive; it would be some time before anyone learned the value of prisoners.)

"I can't let you go," the captain said. "They'll hang me if you're hurt."

"I've been responsible for myself since before you were born," Rogers said. "Also, if we were in the same chain of command you'd be taking orders from me."

"I'll have to clear this with Major Lewis," the captain said tightly.

"Do that." Rogers belted aft where the tunnel party was assembling. A sergeant helped him into a suit of inertron-coated fabric that resembled chain mail but had neutral buoyancy. Belt, air tanks, helmet, and a long rocket rifle completed the gear. The sergeant and Rogers were last to drop out the hatch. Rogers hurried. He didn't want American troops invading those tunnels without him. In the back of his mind were strange thoughts of protecting the girl who looked like Ngo-Lan. It was insane. A stiff old man would be nothing but trouble for the attack teams. But he couldn't put aside the memory of the—female he had seen.

They dropped into cold mountain air. Rogers poised on his jets and found his bearings. The entire top of the mountain was gone and the flying troops were circling the smoothly leveled plateau. There was a round opening where they had found the Han tunnel again.

"You blew up the oldest buildings this side of the pyramids!"

"You better believe it!" The commander's voice rang in Rogers' helmet. "Quiet on this channel except for orders and reports."

Drifting, weapons at ready, the Americans approached that ominous hole in the leveled-off mountain. Rogers and the sergeant held back. "Ultrascope only penetrates two hundred meters," a voice said. "Shielded door at the bottom. Nothing else to that level."

"Side passages?" the sergeant asked.

"Solid rock."

"Duluck, Margot and Swiss, down the tube and try the door. If you're hit get back up and we'll slice off another layer. Rest of you back out of range." The sergeant's voice was cool. A minute passed, then they reported the hatch had yielded and there was more shaft beneath it.

"Scope?" the sergeant asked.

"Side corridors two hundred meters down. I'm at the end of my range, sarge," the ship's operator said.

"Aknol. Point men to the side corridors. Check out and report."

Moments later the scouts reported the storerooms held supplies, but, "No sign of Han, sarge."

"Stay put. 'Rest of you into the hold. Twenty meter intervals."

Rogers was last, where he could accomplish zero if the point were to stumble across Ngo-Lan's trail. Floating gently like Alice down the rabbit hole, he realized what would happen if the Han opened up with dis from below. Armor would protect them from disintegration but in the vacuum, even if they managed to breathe the suddenly falling atmosphere would smash them to the bottom. Lights flickered below him as he dropped.

A memory long forgotten surfaced in his mind: he saw the ageless evil face of the supreme ruler, Emperor Su-Lan, during the months when Rogers was prisoner in his capital. "We shall depart to our new cities deep underground, scattered far and wide through the mountains," he had said. "You will never blast us out of those, even with your most powerful explosives. We shall make our own sunlight in the bowels of the earth. If necessary, we can manufacture pure air—not the germ-laden air of nature. Our underground cities will be heated or cooled as conditions require. Why should we not live underground? We produce all our needs synthetically—nor will you locate us with electronics. All our machinery will be shielded so that no disturbance will exist at the surface."

Obviously, what they had found was the entrance to such an underground complex. Rogers had never imagined it would turn out to be in the Andes. But wasn't that also typical: that the wily Han turned up where least expected?

The cross corridors held clothing, weapons, blocks of preserved food, and drums of water. In addition there was a roomful of communication equipment.

"Sabotaged," a soldier muttered. "If I can find where it was cut . . ." He crouched and began rummaging under the panel. There was a flash and a small explosion; when the soldier fell backward a metal dart was revealed to have been driven through his skull.

"Warn the others," Rogers growled when the sergeant appeared. The sergeant mentioned something about the anality of those unable to refrain from touching strange objects in hostile places but his orders over the command circuit were less pungent.

The Han emperor had said, "From our under-

ground cities we will emerge at leisure to wage
merciless war on you wild men of the forest, until
we have done what our forefathers should have
done: extirpated the last human gene." Rogers
saw the dart in the soldier's forehead. He could
almost see Su-Lan's laughing ghost. "I'll bury you
all before I die!" he had vowed.

"What's that, Marshal?" the sergeant asked,
making Rogers aware that he had been audibly
reminiscing.

"Vengeance, sergeant. Sweeter than luxury,
sweeter than power, sweeter than love of—" He
meant to say 'woman' and it came out 'Wilma.'

"Scope's here. They're setting up."

The portable spy beam did not help much. They
saw down the vertical tunnel. Hundreds of meters
below, in hard rock was another horizontal tunnel
with a single metal rail in the floor. It ran off
beyond the probe's limits in both directions.

"Well, now we know how they got away," Rogers said. His real reason for coming had been to
protect the lovely Han maiden he had glimpsed so
briefly. Eighty three years old! He wondered if
this was some final rally of flagging biology before the inevitable.

"More laterals off the railway," the scopist observed. "but most of them are shielded."

"Is the rail hot?" Rogers asked.

"Can't detect any energy. That doesn't rule out
low level magnetism, but it's not carrying electricity."

"Units two and four occupy the rail tunnel," the
sergeant ordered. "Set up long shooters and blast
anything that moves. Unit one and myself will try
the hatches on the rest of the complex. Hakins is

dead. The rest of you don't go picking up any souvenirs and maybe you'll stay alive. Unit three stay here to guard the scope and the escape route. Move!"

They broke down doors and discovered living quarters. Men whistled. The garrison had garish murals, luxurious divans, full length mirrors, a huge pool of warm water. Over all lay a cloying scent. It took Rogers back to the Han capital in the Rockies.

The sergeant looked a question at him.

"Typical Han," Rogers grunted. He was looking for some hint of female occupancy but with Han it was hard to distinguish. They had pulled out in a hurry, but not in blind panic. There was little personal gear left behind. They paused in what might be the commandant's quarters. Six screens, now dark, lined one wall. Fronting them was a low wide divan with a translucent canopy. A huge mirror flanked by winged dragons filled one end of the room. The other was all closet—folding doors behind a tapestry now pushed aside. Some of the garments seemed feminine. Rogers picked up a silken scarf. Its scent was familiar. He struggled to conceal the quaver in his hands.

"Ultraphone, Marshal."

"Coming, sergeant," He started out of the living quarters and another voice broke in, this time in soprano excitement. "Something in the west tunnel coming this way fast!"

"Loaded," the rocket gunners answered. "Here he comes. Fire!" An instant later an explosion knocked Rogers against the bulkhead. Yellow flame lanced down the tunnel and he heard screams.

"Incoming down the east branch!" the scopist called.

"Got it!" This time the explosion was farther down the tunnel and the gun crew had time to duck. Smoke and the acrid stench of rockets filled the passage.

"Air tanks," the sergeant was yelling when he tripped over Rogers.

"I'm all right," Rogers gasped. "Carry on!" His breath was short and his chest throbbing. Had he taken a whiff of gas or was it just his heart? He staggered to his feet and tried to feel his way through the smoke.

"This end's sealed off." He didn't recognize the voice. Light beams blurred. "Duluck and Margot dead," the sergeant's voice said. West end also sealed. Team three report. I'm sending Swiss up-tunnel. He's wounded. Marshal, you all right?"

"Good as new," Rogers lied.

"Somebody has to take the wounded man top-side."

Rogers struggled to his feet again. "I'll go. Where are you?"

He got the man up out of the smoke and paused to call in. "Ship's been calling you, Marshal," the scopist said.

"Rogers here."

"Niagra HQ wants you." It was the captain's voice.

"Patch it in."

"Marshal, I'm not going to clutter up my command circuit with extra traffic. My men are being killed."

"Correct, captain. I'm coming up with one wounded. Stand by for pickup." He towed the injured trooper to the shaft and jetted upward into cold night air, flying crabwise. He delivered the man to a medtech and staggered down the corridor to communications. His chest and left arm hurt. He asked the comtech for a chair.

"Sure thing, Marshal. You hurt?"

"Just tired."

"Thought I saw blood."

Rogers still had the scarlet Han scarf wrapped around his wrist.

IV

———◆·◆·◆———

Because of the difficult political situation, Congress had requested Rogers' immediate return to North America. The population, according to its anoited leaders, was sick of the expense of the nation's enormous military establishment. Some suspected the reported return of the Han was propaganda for an increased budget whose real purpose was to more tightly grip the world in American hegemony. The senate was more hawkish, being mostly gang bosses and their heirs, but the mass of the people believed they derived no advantage from America's *defacto* empire and found its expense an intolerable burden. Congress needed a personal report from Anthony Rogers, bona fide hero whose word was beyond doubt. If he said there were Han, people would believe, even though they had grown too "sophisticated" for the *Pax Americana*.

Rogers was ready to leave the front. He could help more back in Niagra than making a fool of himself trying to pretend he was young enough to fight in tunnels. One of Major Lewis's ships picked him up. The reinforced assault group was burning through the blocked tunnels. He extracted a promise of reports to his ship as well as to HQ at Puerto Nateles.

But once aboard the rocket to Niagra, Rogers collapsed into a bunk and slept till they landed. Anxious bosses were waiting to brief him. Fortunately, he was not to address Congress until noon next day.

Rogers was still imposing despite gray hair, and his enormous prestige was accentuated by the plain uniform without insignia that was his trademark. Recordings of that speech are all too available.

He assured the federated gangs from Alaska down to the silted remains of the Canal that the Han had indeed returned, "Had been lurking beneath the earth of our neighbor to the south." Briefly, and with touching modesty he told of his encounter with his old enemies. And oh, how they thrilled at the thought of an eighty three year year old hero bringing down the first ship!

The suntanned old man was still the hero they had seen so many times on historical documentaries. "Against poison gas, booby traps, dis beams and robot killer ships our young Americans are even now locked in life-or-death struggle," he summed up. He told of the vast underground city the Han had been abuilding even as Lo-Tan was destroyed in the last war. He was the only human who had seen it. He warned that others might lurk beneath the soil of Peru.

Rogers convinced them the Han were real and

not a warmonger's hoax. Congress voted that same day for greater arms budgeting and unlimited deployment south of the Canal. Nobody asked if the South Americans wanted protection. They should be grateful—especially since American policy had long prevented—often with force—other countries from fielding their own armies.

News from Peru was not encouraging. Operation Rathole continued, with the American and Peruvian forces boring their slow way into the unbelievable tunnel complex, facing explosives, gas, and flooding. Few Han were found. None were taken. The defenses were always automatic or remote controlled. The Han seemed strong on new technology but short on manpower, which was odd since they had never before been innovative. In three days of grubbing through their tunnels the Americans had lost a hundred men and women—and still no city or major base had been found.

(In Puerto Natales a young man's broken arm was healing. Perhaps a young woman's heart was healing. Will Holcomb watched her face. "Don't understand one word I say, do you, Yolanda?" Brown eyes regarded him. She smiled and her fingers crept into his hand. To bridge the gulf of difference in language they had difference in sex.)

Rogers was in the Citadel when General Gordon called. The general took a chair and apologized for calling in person. "This is more than a vidplate matter, Tony."

Rogers sat behind his massive desk. There were no windows in the fortress and he had decorated the walls to suit himself. Behind the desk hung two large paintings: one of the Rockies seen from the air; the other a reproduction from Rogers' previous existence—Washington Crossing the Delaware. Some wondered but none dared ask why there was no memento of Wilma. The other walls held respectively a vidscreen and a map with a small red pin in the Andes east of Puerto Nateles. "Bull, you wouldn't have tracked me down if it weren't important," Rogers assured the caller, "I know that."

"We need your support."

"The South American Business?"

The general nodded. "Isolationists and cowards are bad enough. Now some so-called intellectuals are bitching. Seems some of their research money was diverted into mobilization."

"Fools!" Rogers snapped. "How much research would they do under the Han?"

"You know it and I know it, Tony. Can you talk to some of those professors?"

"If you think it'll help. Who are they?"

"Dr. Ruth Harris at Niagra University, for openers. Do you know her?"

"Sounds familiar. Should I?"

"She's a Deering."

These slips of memory bothered Rogers. "Long time ago," he said. "She was just a child." Since Wilma had died he had not kept much track of his in-laws. He knew that at his age people expected him to be forgetful but he didn't like to live up to their expectations.

"Should I invite her here or can you go to the university?"

"I'll go. Won't hurt to show her a little deference. Besides, I've never seen any of our new schools except the military academy."

"You'll find this one different," General Gordon said.

One difference was that the heavy North American forest had not been cleared for parade grounds and athletic fields. University buildings hid among trees, nearly invisible as the two man swooper came down onto a narrow strip. Rogers dismissed the pilot and belted off, following a blazed trail through the trees until he found the Physical Sciences Building.

The students seemed cleancut, serious—and very young—military life had inured Rogers to fuzzycheeked combat troops but these students seemed like children! Perhaps it was because they were not grim. Dr. Harris was waiting.

At least forty, he judged. She wore glasses and had gray streaks in long brown hair. He thought wryly of a time when forty had seemed senile, wrung of all passion. Now he could see her as she was: delicate, mature—and very pretty. She wore a white lab coat but under it was a welltailored, formfitting blouse and short skirt which revealed a body with no visible defects. Rogers abruptly realized she had dressed up for him. God, if he were only . . . would twenty years be younger enough?

Ruth Harris had been in love with Anthony Rogers since she was five years old, as had every girl in North America just after the war. His picture was everywhere. He was King Arthur, brave warrior, mysterious man from the past, heroic leader. Nor did it hurt that he was nearly six feet in an age of undernourished shorties, muscular, handsome, and had a boyish grin. Oh, they had all loved him; Ruth still did.

She had met him once as a child but he had never really seen her. Even then she had sensed that while the fiercely possessive Wilma existed there would be no chance for. . . for anything. As if he would even think—with Wilma watching he'd better not!

But Wilma was gone now and if he was in his eighties he was still a man and he was going to notice her now. He'd damn well better or there was going to be trouble. She had donned a strictly severe manner but suddenly she was blushing.

She knew why he was here. She was determined to get back that appropriation. But she was also a grown up girl meeting her childhood idol. Her heart raced.

"Marshal Rogers? I'm Ruth Harris."

"Hello, Dr. Harris. My friends still call me Tony." The boyish charm had not eroded.

They visited the laboratories first. Rogers was gadgeteer enough not to be awed by equipment, and he was able to ask mostly intelligent questions and understood at least some of the answers. He made appropriately admiring comment on a huge vacuum chamber, the particle accelerator, the atomic pile, and a reconstructed Han power broadcaster.

"Energy," she said, picking up a small black cube, "is the one thing the Han seem to have plenty of. We've always concentrated on portable rechargable power sources instead of tapping their broadcast power and maybe having them turn it off at the wrong moment. Of course in the past this limited us to puny power sources. Not anymore, though; this battery is really just a pool of electrons separated from their protons."

"A fistful of real power," Rogers conceded. He had done his homework. "Your work, I believe?"

"Separating the fundamental aspects of matter is what we're strong on. Actually, though, I'm not sure if I've done something original, or just made an obvious improvement on Han technology." She brushed hair back. "But making it work isn't as important as understanding how it works."

"Why?" Rogers wondered.

"Didn't you say in one of your speeches that a little knowledge is dangerous? We have a whole society using jump belts, antigravity—forces nobody really understands."

"Someday I'll tell you another ancient story about a girl named Pandora."

"I know it."

"How could you?"

"When you were—younger—you often made cryptic remarks. Did you think young and curious hero worshipers would not spend lifetimes tracking down your every allusion?"

Rogers had never thought about it at all.

"Pandora didn't know what was in the box. Neither do we. But each time I peek in I see more of which way those fangs will snap."

"You frighten me."

"Not half so much as you frighten me," Dr. Harris said grimly. She put the battery down. "Virus lab next."

She conducted him through bio labs and the

astronomy department where photos of Mars through a twenty inch reflector graced one wall. "Have you never wished to go to another planet?" she asked.

Rogers controlled himself. He visited the site of the slowly growing space ship exactly as often as he could not get out of it. He started to say something politic, then changed his mind. Why not be honest just once? "What on Earth for? Even if it becomes possible," he said, "To what end? Earth has a fraction of the population it had when I left my own era in 1927. It may be thousands of years before we run short of land. And with the Han killing us off . . ." He left it dangling.

They passed into a small office where flowers crowded a desk piled high with reports. Dr. Harris's lab assistant made tea and left them alone. Ruth moved her chair so the desk was not between them and crossed her legs. Sunlight filtered through trees into the room. "The new edict from Niagra will strip us of a third of our staff to work on war projects," she began bluntly. "We have projects and experiments half completed."

"Who pays?" Rogers interrupted.

"Partly the government," she acknowledged. "Instructors and students are supported by their gangs. They spend a few years, then leave."

"And you?"

"My family can afford to keep me working here."

He had forgotten that the Northeast was experimenting with capitalism again. The Deering clan, to which Dr. Harris and *Wilma* belonged, had managed as usual to land on their feet. When he had awakened in this era Rogers had been horrified to find the gangs had no concept of private property. All that was changing, now that the human race was no longer on the run.

"It's not that I begrudge our government its citizens' services in a crisis," she went on. "But you know as well as I that once the military takes something over I'll never get it back."

"No doubt for the same reason you don't want to give it up."

"Oh, I'm human too," Ruth said, tossing her hair back, "but, Tony, can't you see our purpose here is different? It's more than a power struggle: we've just begun to think again—to dream, speculate, yearn for understanding after centuries under the heel of the Han. I don't want the university to lose that!"

Rogers was more moved by the woman than by her argument. "Some compromise," he found himself saying, "in which University people lend their time to military projects but come back after, say, two years?"

"There's another problem you can help us with," she went on. "There's the science and technology of the Han."

"The Han were a degenerate race," Rogers said flatly. "Their knowledge was old. That's why we defeated them when war finally came."

"You defeated them."

"I had a part in it."

"The point is, Tony," She leaned closer and looked him squarely in the eyes, "they had science we didn't have, and still don't understand. They seemed weak and degenerate, but look what they did! Tony, during your time as prisoner in Lo-Tan, did you see any hint of research or scholarship?"

Rogers thought back. The city had been a marvel—but an inefficient, constantly breaking down marvel. The Han knew they were a race of destiny, though destined for what was less clear to them. They lived in luxury and did little work since production was automated. Only the military and the repairmen were truly busy. Females circulated. Males lolled in front of vidplates and rarely left their apartments. It had been a highly stratified society, with an aristocracy of blood contending for control with the army, the air crews, and the powerful repairmen. He described this to Ruth Harris.

In vain she picked at his memory for science other than the technology she already knew. "If they had things like the rep and the dis ray, why didn't they go farther? It's almost as if they didn't invent those things themselves, but had them given to them."

"Given by whom?" Rogers worried. "Are we going to run into some still more powerful race in the future?"

"The Han showed little understanding of what they had," she said. "Tony, if only all of you hadn't destroyed everything—cities, machincery, records, libraries . . ."

"It was war," Rogers said uneasily. He remembered the genocidal fury with which American forces attacked the Han at every turn. Even his lovely wife, Wilma. Especially Wilma.

"The dis ray," Ruth continued. "You all, Han included, assumed it destroyed matter. It was only later that a few of us trained in physics asked where all the energy was going. Look at the power from our atomic pile, which only transforms a tiny fraction of matter to energy. The "curtain of fire" the Han put around their cities would have cooked the planet."

She filled his cup and settled back, looking at Rogers from deep brown eyes. "We tested the beam on a piece of armor plate in the vacuum chamber. The iron disappeared all right but the chamber floor got a coating of iron dust which settled within a minute; all the ray does is redistribute molecules. We got some of the iron back, almost all of the sample had been redistributed outside the chamber."

"I remember," Tony said. "The dis is an excellent weapon since it vaporizes everything in its path. But I guess you can't really violate the old law of Conservation of Matter."

"Not exactly," the woman said. "But it takes some rearrangement of our concept of the continuity of space, since the particles are transported—our teams prefer their own word, "teleported"—considerable distances almost instantaneously. Anyway, the question of where the molecules go—they do not cross the intervening space—and how they come back remains unanswered. Unless the Han knew and the records were destroyed."

"What difference does it make, as long as it works?"

"We don't understand it." She almost said "I don't understand it." She was disappointed that Rogers could not see this. If he were younger . . . but Rogers, the hero, had always been a man of action and not given to contemplation.

"Suppose," she said, "you didn't have to break down the ray's target to component molecules. Suppose you could teleport whole objects . . ."

"People?"

"We don't know yet."

He thought a moment. The setting sun filled the forest outside with orange light. Inside it was getting dark.

"Alright," he said, "I'll do what I can to keep your university budgeted."

"Only because you see some military advantage to the research," she sighed.

"Naturally. But I do see your viewpoint. Try to see mine. The Han will not split hairs as they kill us."

"I believe you. Now, this new war of yours—"

"I thought it was our—the Human Race's—war," Rogers replied drily.

Ruth had the grace to blush. "I mean this war you're . . . fighting. It's another opportunity to study the Han. Can you persuade them not to destroy everything, not slaughter every prisoner?"

Rogers remembered the girl in the tunnel. "I'll do everything I can," he said intensely. "We've taken one prisoner but he's just a common soldier."

"Oh? Where was he captured?"

"In the Peruvian Andes. He was part of the tunnel entrance garrison. I stunned him with a near miss."

"You?" Suddenly she was five again—there was no one like Tony . . . her Tony. She controlled herself. "Can you arrange for the people here to question him?"

"I suppose so." Rogers did not know that the air crew had already made a foray into Han science by seeing if the captured soldier could land from four thousand meters with neither armor nor belt.

"Can I ask you another favor?" As she smiled at him Rogers' vision of the slender Han girl faded. He grinned his famous grin.

"Talk to one of our biologists over in the next building."

"Why not?"

Dr. Wolsky was short and plump and wore a short white beard. He led his visitors through endless ranks of glass boxes and sleeping rats. Wolsky seemed the only one in the lab who was awake. Each rat was in a separate box with temperature, gas content, and electrical flux recording on instruments built into its front. Like a puppet, each animal had fine wires strung from head, chest and limbs that led out from the top of the box. The little scientist pointed out the undulant traces of brain waves, heart activity, respiration, blood pressure, urine formation, and muscle tone as they squiggled across graph paper.

"Very impressive," Rogers said. "But what does it tell you?"

"I watch them sleep."

"Sleep?"

"Not normal sleep. I am trying for suspended animation."

Rogers felt his hackles rise. Ruth Harris gave him an embarrassed little smile. "Show Marshal Rogers the results," she suggested.

An assistant produced notebooks of handwritten observations in different colored inks. "Here's a moderate success." Wolsky pointed to a page of indecipherable abbreviations. "This rat lived three years."

Rogers thought of his own awakening after five hundred. "Woke up after three years? How long do rats live?"

"Not woke up. Died. They all die."

"But—"

"I know," Wolsky interrupted. "Why do you think I study this? Your five century sleep is inexplicable. I have been working fifteen years."

Rogers stared. "I always thought radioactivity—"

"Not likely. But even that I tried. Radiation does not bring life; in small amounts it does nothing; in larger quantities it sometimes generates carcinomas, in very large amounts radiation kills outright."

Ruth put a hand on Rogers' shoulder. "What Wol is working up to is that you're unique. He wants to study you."

Rogers looked at rows of sleeping, dying rats. "Like that?"

"No, no! Not into the sleep. But perhaps there is about you something special—brain waves, heart, blood, metabolism . . ."

"How much time are we talking about, Doc?"

"A day. Maybe two."

"I can spare a day if it would help."

"Thank you, thank you, Marshal." He seized Rogers' hand. "Let me arrange for physical recordings first."

Ruth looked at Rogers. "I thank you too," she

said. "Wol is too excited to know what to say. While he's testing I'll arrange for you to stay in the dorm."

"Do you think he's going to learn anything?"

She shrugged. "To learn which things are not possible is progress. But Wol and I are in total disagreement. He believes—I guess you do too— that something got into your body and preserved it. I think that's impossible."

"What do you think happened?" Though he was old, Rogers' life had been so full of action that until now he had never taken the time to ponder that question. Now he realized that he had simply labeled the phenomenon "Miracle: not to be questioned" and filed it away in his mind. Such were the joys of extroversion.

"It must have been some process that altered time in a limited area."

"Time travel?"

"Logical inconsistencies make that absurd. But something happened five centuries ago."

"Was anything ever found in that abandoned mine?"

"No one knows where it is except you."

"No one has investigated?" Now that he thought about it, he was incredulous.

"Nobody could ever find it."

"Should have asked me. Would it help if I located it?"

"Tony, I don't think you understand how important you are. Of course it would help. No one ever dared ask you, that's all. Talk to Wolsky. Here he comes." She smiled. "I'll rescue you in an hour. Shall we have dinner together?"

"If you have time." It had been a long afternoon

and Rogers was tired. He managed a smile and thought of a time when he would have risen more gallantly to a lady's invitation.

V

━━━━━━━━━◆━◆━◆━━━━━━━━━

As the Americans advanced through the Han tunnels they periodically burned away the ultron shielding, thus permitting the circling airships to follow their progress. Gradually Major Lewis's reinforced fleet spread east through the mountains, mirroring in the air the underground invasion. While this did not interfere with communications because of the highpowered ultraphones, it did mean his fleet had been spread thin. On Entallador's map the handful of blue pins now stretched two hundred kilometers.

Then the Han struck. The force penetrating the Rat Hole had reached an intersection of six tunnels when the Heaven Born attacked with rep ray armed ground cars guided and powered by single metal rails. Lewis leaned over the map. "How deep are those devils?"

"Half a kilometer," an aide reported.

"Who's doing air cover?"

"Norris, sir."

Lewis switched channels on his helmet phone.

"Captain Norris, this is Blue Central. What's the terrain below you?"

"Wide valley. Heavy jungle, no sign of habitation."

"Good. To the east of the troopers' present position cut down through the tunnels and interdict them."

"Aknol. We'll have to descend to ground level."

"I'm sending Units eight and eleven for air cover. Those units acknowledge."

Both ships reported and changed position. This left gaps since Lewis was sending in the ships closest to the battle site.

"Unit six in tunnel three reports Han," an ultraphonist called. "They're using grenades and slug throwers."

"Tell him he has to hold until we can cut through behind them," Lewis snarled as he studied the map, a hurried pasteup of topographical surveys, each slightly out-of-scale with its neighbor. He was having trouble with the coordinates.

"*Mayor* Lewis," Entallador interrupted, "If my *guerrilleros* can be transported we will hit behind them."

"How many have you recruited?"

"Almost two hundred," the *pandillero* said. "No heavy arms, but with belts, some guns, *y muchos machetes.*"

"Haven't got a ship can carry that many," Lewis sighed.

"Two small rockets on patrol, sir," interrupted a new voice. "We don't have to load the troops.

They've got belts and if they're as tough as the ones I've met, we can tow them."

Lewis looked up. It was a tall American airman. At first he didn't know him, then he saw the arm slung inside the lieutenant's jacket. "I'm short on crew," Lewis said. "Are you well enough to fly?"

"Sure," Holcomb said. "I won't be doing anything fancy with men strung out behind me."

So it was that when Han ships erupted from the northern mountains an hour later Holcomb was aloft in a two man scout rocket, trailing a "kite tail" of two hundred men hooked onto 150 meters of ultron line. Hedgehopping slowly, he had just come into sight of the truncated top of Cerro del Huanco. The ultraphone was suddenly jammed with excited and conflicting reports. Three ships began to report a wave of enemy aircraft. Not one managed to complete its broadcast.

Not knowing the enemy's location, Holcomb continued his slow hedgehopping toward Gemelo Pass. The rocket on station wheeled and shrieked off north. Holcomb scanned the sky for the cigar shape of a Han ship. A gentle breeze bent treetops and tugged fitfully on his tow line. Nothing else moved. None of his cargo spoke Anglish. He called Puerto Nateles and asked for an interpreter. He got Entallador.

"Your bandidos make too good a target. If the Han show I'm going to drop the line. Tell them if that happens, to scatter and I'll try to draw off any enemy ships." Holcomb's ship had two light rockets, one at each wing tip. After they were gone, he had one fifty-calibre machine gun—or he could crash-land and throw rocks. No real difference between the last two options.

He moved steadily to avoid whipping the tow and tried to make sense out of the chatter on the ultraphone. There were several Han aloft, engaged by at least two American units. Still the sky ahead remained clear. Crossing the pass, he had to speed up lest the constant wind snarl the tow but finally he dropped into the calm of the eastern valley. Holcomb scanned the horizon. He was not tuned to the local ground channel so he missed the outbreak of Español from his own towline. A moment later an anguished Entallador broke in. "¡Pronto, teniente—atrás!"

"Huh?"

"Quick, lieutenant, behind you!"

It was high in the sky, coming out of the sun. Holcomb could not turn without fouling the tow line. "Tell them to drop off!" he yelled. A thin blue beam flickered.

The dis ray cut the tow line. Four Peruvians vanished, vaporized, their impervious jump belts sailing off into the sky.

Holcomb cut loose. He did not have time to maneuver but without the drag his small ship accelerated just enough for a small round craft to plummet scant meters behind him. It tore through multilayered jungle and a mushroom of orange flame erupted. The explosion tore one of his wingtip rockets loose. "Drop ship!" he yelled. "Missed me and went in."

"Must be what got Blue Five," answered headquarters.

Holcomb powered up over the burning jungle. Looking back, he saw his Peruvians drifting down into the trees around the area of the explosion. He could tell from their uncontrolled flight that many were dead. He peered through the ultron cockpit bubble for more attackers. "Lost some men," he reported. "Others may be safe unless . . . yep. Here comes a rep ray ship."

Suspended on ground effect rays, a long airship came stalking like a spider over the eastern mountains. Holcomb struggled onehandedly to drive his underpowered scout up where he could not be "stepped on" and would have to deal only with dis beams.

He had to draw the Han away from the helpless troops cowering in the jungle where tree trunks and bamboo exploded like artillery as rep and dis rays competed to create chaos. It would also be helpful to the cause if he could get himself and his borrowed ship back intact. But the fact that he was not in the Eagle now accounted for most of his trouble. This ship flew low and slow, making up for it with an almost total lack of maneuverability now that one wingtip rocket was gone. He had to fire the other just to regain balance. Jigging to avoid another drop ship, he angled toward the enemy and fired his single remaining offensive tool and watched it burst ineffectually against the larger ship. Then dis flared in his path, caught and held him. His inertron shielding protected him from disruption, but the rays followed him, keeping him always in a pocket of outrushing air which starved his jets—and the cabin air supply came through shielded baffles.

Holcomb's head swam. The world closed down as his peripheral vision went. The instruments before him seemed to recede from his good arm

similarly to the way his ship was receding from
the surface of earth: firing both of his missiles the
ship had positive buoyancy—and no motors to
keep it down. He gulped air and grunt breathed,
struggling for vision. Somehow he found strength
to move the switch that sealed the baffles and
turned on tanked air. There had to be a better way
to design these ships.

When he could breathe again Holcomb made a
few well-chosen remarks about the state of en-
gineering in America. He tried controls but the
ship did not respond. Nearly a minute passed
while he floated to the limit of the Han rays and
emerged into air again. His own dis jets, even free
from Han bombardment, could find little air at
this altitude; much higher and he would never
have come down.

Moving on angled rep rays, the Han ship now
ignored him as it stalked over the green valley and
through the pass.

"One Han coming through Gemelo Pass," Holcomb phoned. "I can't stop him."

"Holcomb!" He did not recognize the voice.
"All units near you are in business. You're on
your own."

"Hey Puerto Nateles, he's headed right for you.
You guys better evacuate!" Good God, he thought,
Yolanda and old Entallador are there—and they
won't leave until everyone else has been moved: it
would take hours; they had minutes.

How to bring down a ship almost impervious to
small-caliber artillery? He and Rogers had tipped
over one Han robot but that had been done by
applying force from two sides simultaneously,
and would not have succeeded without his near-

suicidal ramming. Now he was alone. As he began
to gain on the stalking Han raider Holcomb
searched feverishly for ideas.

Down on the coast Entallador's dis ray projectors had proven ineffective against the downed
Han's hatches. Those doors had only opened to
explosives. Maybe this ship had no dis ray shielding. Unlikely but he had to try something. He
studied the controls on the dis powered jet of his
own ship. It was set for nitrogen at two hundred
meters, which meant he was boring a tunnel in the
air before him, drawing 80% of the atmosphere
into his jet chambers. This compressed gas jetting
from the rear accelerated the ship's progress into
the constant vacuum ahead of it.

There was a control to change the dis jet setting;
also a red latch over the interlocking focus over-
ride. This was to prevent clogging,possibly blowing up his jets with a too rich mass from devoured
solids. By narrowing the focus to a pinpoint this
ship could fly underwater—for short distances.
At close range the dis would attack anything—
even metal! But a pilot did not tamper casually
with that red latch over the interlock. Holcomb's
mind weighed his ship and his own value against
Puerto Nateles' inhabitants. Then his heart
weighed it against one of them. He diddled the
interlock and dived!

The Han responded with dis but Holcomb
momentumed through, lashed the Han ship with
his ray and—nothing happened. "Gobblasten-
dammet!"

"Message garbled. Please repeat."

"Street in Stockholm where my ancestors
lived," Holcomb growled, and switched off his

helmet. So they were shielded after all. Well it had been a faint hope. He widened focus and picked up speed.

He whipped past the Han cigar-ship again. Firing his autopopgun in frustrated fury. The Han flicked a dis ray at the annoyance but did not stop: bigger game in sight.

Holcomb pulled out of his dive and hovered— something was different about the Han . . . but what? Wait! There were shiny streaks on the flat gray surface where his shots had struck. Unless they were traces from his own rounds, he had breached the shielding. Or had he just polished it? One way to find out.

By this time, Nateles had come in view and high explosive rockets were bursting around him. His ship shuddered. The Han crusied on.

"Hold fire!" Holcomb yelled uselessly. "Give me a chance first." At least the Han ship was preoccupied with answering ground fire. He swung behind the attacker and as bluish dis probed the outskirts of the port he got alongside. Using part of his power to brake, but keeping the dis engines on full and trained on the side of the Han cruiser, he moved in, almost but not quite motionless relative to the aggressor. As his ship nosed the enemy, throwing him against his seat belts, he saw enemy metal begin to dissolve where the shielding was scarred. Brute momentum did the rest.

Dis holed the Han. There was a muffled explosion and his scout was thrown free, tumbling. The Han dipped and swooped across the sky like a berserk scoop-shovel. Two rep ray batteries were gone. It tumbled end over end into a hillside two kilometers outside of town. Holcomb couldn't believe his luck; according to plan, he was supposed to be *inside* the enemy vessel—boring from within, as it were—when it went down.

The woods were thick and pathless. After an hour Rogers was ready to admit he was lost. "I'd forgotten how many weeks I spent grubbing about before I met Wilma," he said. "I'd given up ever seeing a human face again."

"Also the vegetation has changed since then," Wolsky said. "Try to recall the lay of the land—hills, valleys, streams. Meanwhile—" He consulted a map whose blank spaces they had laboriously filled. "We put heavy equipment here." He gestured toward the sky sled being towed by two graduate students. "Then, while the light lasts, each of us takes one vector and explores, say, two miles."

Rogers sat in the clearing Wolsky had chosen for their camp. All this wilderness in the middle of Pennsylvania! It belonged, he knew, to the Wyoming gang, controlled now mostly by the Ciardi and Deering clans, to which he was allied by marriage.

"What're we looking for, Marshal?" one of the students asked.

"It was once a mine," the man from the past replied. "I awoke in the shaft but the lateral behind me was gone. I had to work my way up a long tunnel, so I must still have been well below the surface."

"Anything special about the tunnel or the rock?"

"The rock was soft; not like the strata above.

There was a coal seam."

"Nothing we could see from the surface?"

"Nothing but the mine-shaft entrance. The head-frame must have rotted away centuries ago."

"Needle in a haystack," the student muttered.

"I know," Rogers agreed. "Unless there's still some radioactivity."

His personal pilot joined them. "Whatever it is, sir, it's either small or well shielded. We scanned the whole area with ultrascope. I think we ought to try farther down the valley."

Rogers shook his head. "I trust my memory more than that. I'd wandered fifty miles down-valley before I met Wilma. It's here somewhere."

"If it's shielded," the student said, "That gives more weight to Dr. Harris's theory that we're look-ing for some kind of space-time anomaly." A rab-bit broke cover almost at their feet and bounded away.

"How appropriate!" Rogers chuckled. "I do hope he isn't late."

Pilot and student stared uncomprehendingly.

Embarrassed at being caught in a thoroughly uncharacteristic moment of whimsy, Rogers ig-nored their bafflement and returned to the subject at hand. "I admit the whole thing seems totally unlikely." That was understating it. When he en-dured the insomnia of age it sometimes seemed none of it had ever happened. Maybe it had just seemed a good story for a friendless stranger to tell in exchange for a meal. But Wilma had been real. Boy, had Wilma ever been real!

Two hours later a student reported an anomaly

in magnetometer reading up a small defile that fed into the Wyoming Valley. Rogers belted skyward and circled until someone signaled with a flag flapping atop an inertron line. The area did not look at all familiar, but it had been fifty years. Then they found the slanting tunnel.

The party was torn between excitement and caution. Rogers wanted to burn through the ground with dis. He was sure he remembered his temporary tomb at considerable depth. Wolsky was adamantly opposed for fear of disturbing whatever it was they were investigating. To proceed slowly, reinforcing the tunnel at every step was obviously proper. But nobody wanted to wait.

"Look," Rogers said. "I got out once. I'll just walk down. You can follow me on the scope and we'll be in continuous contact."

"No!" Wolsky cried. "Somebody goes with you. You both wear helmets in case of gas. You must monitor radioactivity all the way down. We will keep an ultron line tied to you all the way. I have included one two thousand meters long in our equipment."

Rogers insisted on going. The others drew straws. The inquisitive student, Ducall, won. As they suited up Rogers began to feel the thrill that preceded any adventure. Suppose there was a hole in time back to 1927? Would he be able to step through into his own past? Would anybody believe him if he did? Well, he could show them a thing or two! He chuckled at the thought.

They had walked, climbed, and dropped over five hundred meters when their helmet ultraphones went dead. They stopped and played lights around the narrow sloping passage. Nothing but bare rock streaked with efflorescence. They walked back up until they were in contact with the surface again.

Wolsky was wildly excited that they had found something—anything. The ultrascopist reported that both spelunkers had disappeared from the screen and then reappeared.

"There must be a shielding field in here," Rogers said. "We'll go on."

"Maybe," Wolsky squeaked, "you should wait until we can get a larger party down."

"We're going on," Rogers said. "We must be near bottom by now."

"We don't want to lose all contact," Wolsky protested. "Wait until we can set up some sort of wired radio."

Rogers laughed. "Going to reinvent the telephone? Maybe we can relay ultraphone up to you." He took off his helmet, set the controls to pick up and retransmit, and put it on the tunnel floor at the extreme range of surface equipment. Back down with Ducall, he had the student call the surface. They were getting through the anomaly.

"Just the same," Wolsky relayed, "I am sending a second party down as far as the shield in case you need assistance."

Rogers and his companion resumed their cautious descent.

"Marshal," Ducall said a moment later, "Why don't you take my helmet? It'll put you direct with Dr. Wolsky and also protect you from any gas or stale air."

"I'm not afraid of bad air," Rogers said cheerfully, "Not after 1927 in Pittsburgh. And you can talk to Wolsky." He paused. "How about radioactivity? Anything yet?"

"Just normal background."

"Strange. It was quite hot down here the first time."

"You know, Marshal, the real miracle is not that you've lived five hundred years."

"Oh?"

"By now you should be one solid mass of cancer."

"In 1927 we thought radioactivity cured cancer."

"So does a dis ray," Ducall said. "Hey, what's this?"

They had reached a cave-in. From under the rubble came a bluish gleam. While Ducall reported Rogers started to clear away the rock. He uncovered a metallic surface covering the tunnel floor. It was slightly convex: its shape would extrapolate into a large sphere. "Instruments?" Rogers asked.

"Not a peep." Ducall approached the blue dome and cautiously touched it with his boot. He bent and rapped it with his gloved knuckles. No sound. "Feels solid," he said, and rested his hand on the surface.

Rogers reached out. The smooth hemisphere vanished before his fingertips. He and Ducall were falling into the sudden space beneath their feet. The younger man yipped. Rogers flipped and landed on his feet. His belt prevented any real fall, but still, Rogers was surprised to discover he was quavering from the exertion. Suddenly the chamber was alight.

"Jackpot!" Ducall cried. It was another of those terms this poor pokerless age had gleaned from Rogers' early speeches.

The chamber was small, and crowded with cables, bus bars, and enigmatic cabinets. In the exact center were two cot-sized padded tables, centered beneath a light of operating-room intensity. The machinery had no knobs, switches, dials, or other visible controls. Nothing happened.

"Lost contact with Wolsky again," Ducall flipped the switch on his helmet back and forth. Rogers glanced up. The ceiling of the chamber was still open.

"Shielding of some sort," he said.

"Does this place look familiar?" Ducall asked.

Rogers shook his head. "I may have been here . . . I regained consciousness in the shaft. . . . The thing did open to my touch. . . . I—" He stopped, a strange, intent look on his face. "I—"

"Something wrong, Marshal?" the young man asked. To his horror, instead of answering Rogers clutched his chest and groaned. His face was pale and a line of sweat appeared on his lip.

"What is it?" Ducall repeated frantically as Rogers went away.

As Ducall eased Rogers to the floor he realized with growing horror that the rumors about the old man's bad heart were true. He felt for a pulse and could find none.

Ducall still wore his air tank and helmet though Rogers had taken his off. He wondered if a gas pocket had provoked the heart attack, then realized his own helmet was open. He was breathing the same air. Rogers was undoubtedly dead by now. Should he race back to the surface? He didn't know any first aid. He remembered something about striking the chest of a person with heart failure but with his luck he'd just break the old man's ribs.

For lack of more constructive activity, he put Rogers' limp but inertron-light body on one of the raised pallets in the middle of the chamber. There was a hum as lights dimmed. Before Ducall could move a blue glow filled the air and Rogers seemed to dissolve into a dark skeleton suspended above the cot. Then the space above the cot filled with an opaque glistening surface. The light brightened again.

Ducall stared down at the shiny capsule shape where Rogers had been. He touched the shield with his fingers. He struck it. No sound. What was he ever going to tell Dr. Wolsky?

Dr. Wolsky was delighted. His suspicions were confirmed; Rogers' five hundred year sleep was linked to some sort of life-support system buried in the abondoned mine.

"But how do you know he's even in there?" Ducall protested. "I saw him dissolve right down to the bones. Maybe that's his tombstone—or some kind of substitute mass to balance a teleportation equation. We have no idea what's really happening!"

Wolsky sobered for an instant, then his cheerful mien returned. "My boy, even a scientist must accept some things on faith. Rogers will return."

Ducall wondered how he could have spent his life among lunatics and only now have it brought to his attention.

Wolsky promptly ordered all the apparatus he

could think of from the university to study the newly discovered chamber. It was only when he remembered to call Dr. Harris that other implications of the event were brought to his attention. Dr. Wolsky was, after all, a scientist.

"Wol, where is he?" Ruth asked for the third time.

"Well, we think he is into the machine locked somewhere."

"Can you see him?"

"No. He is enclosed by some kind of force we cannot penetrate with ultrascope. I am reluctant to attack with energy beams for fear of destroying the machinery or setting off some other protective device."

"Wol, is he—alive?"

"My dear, how can I say? Ducall thinks he had a heart attack. I'm asking for a medico to fly out with the supplies. . . ."

That was spoken to an empty screen; Ruth was on her way.

Twenty four hours later however, she returned disconsolate to the university: the field defied everything, including dis ray, and the scientists were reluctant to attack the machinery in the room before they had some understanding of it. Dr. Harris flew to Niagra immersed in an emotional stew compounded of love, grief, patriotism and self interest. The public could wait but the military had to know that Rogers was gone, disappeared, as it were, while participating in some sort of scientific experiment.

She was reminded of a story Rogers had once told of some alchemist whom the devil had snatched away to the accompaniment of a clap of thunder. How had the assistants beaten off the witch hunters after their leader blew himself up experimenting with gunpowder? How was she going to explain Uncle Tony's disappearance?

While she was trying to mentally recapitulate the feet of the master's followers who had saved their bacon, word arrived from Pennsylvania that the field had collapsed and Anthony Rogers had emerged—alive!

The pain was gone. He waited a long minute to be sure. Yes. His instinct for action took over. He opened his eyes, braced himself to leap. The chamber was empty but he could hear voices. In the dim light he saw machines looming bulky and massive in the gloom. He lay on a narrow table, hands extended. He grasped the sides, lifted his head, and looked down. He still wore the same gray uniform he had been wearing when the pain hit and he blacked out. How long ago? Five hundred years? Was he destined to progress into the future like some H. G. Wells character in half-millenium jumps? Someone entered. With a feeling akin to disappointment he recognized Dr. Wolsky. "How long have I been here?"

"Three and a half days."

Rogers sat and swung his legs over the side of the cot. "I feel fine," he assured Wolsky. "Is this what kept me in suspended animation way back when?"

"Probably. But still we do not understand what it does, how, or most importantly, why?" Rogers studied the ranked cabinets and cables that led to the pair of cots. "Come away!" Wolsky said, "before it seals you up again and this time we can't get you out."

"Did you break it open? I'd hoped I'd slept another five hundred years."

"Do you feel as if you had? No, we could not get near you. We even tried *dis*. You came out spontaneously. Come outside and we'll make some tests. Ducall thought you had a heart attack."

"I remember the pain," Rogers said as they jumped into the cave above. "I feel fine—like a new man." Students and techs clustered, shouting congratulations and amazement. Wolsky waved them off. "Come to the surface and let me examine you."

There was a camp outside the mine entrance. Wolsky led Rogers into the largest tent and hastily gathered an examination kit. "Strip off your clothes."

Rogers started to obey, then stopped. "Doc, look at me!"

"I've been doing that. Go on, go on. Take your clothes off.

Rogers was staring at his bare chest and arms. Gone were the brown keratoses of incipient senility. Under a smooth youthful skin lay firm muscles. With trembling hands Rogers pulled off his helmet. His hair was thick and healthy. His hands were no longer wrinkled claws. His veins were firm. He clenched his fists and the life force surged.

"Doc, how old am I?"

"Yes," Wolsky said, evasively as a cornered politician. "Let me find you a mirror. We must run many tests. The transformation is remarkable."

Rogers was fascinated by his image: wrinkles and lines gone; muscle tone firm; hairline restored. Rogers gasped: "I'm young again!" He dropped the mirror. He advanced on the heavy center pole of the tent and threw his weight against it. The tent swayed.

"Hey!" Wolsky yelled.

Laughing, Rogers tore the pole from the ground, swung it, ripped canvas. The tent pole snapped. Ducall was among those who extricated Dr. Wolsky from the collapsed tent. Perhaps the older man would hereafter be less inclined to accept things on faith alone: it looked like the Rogers who had entered the tunnel was well and truly gone!

VI

As Holcomb struggled from the wreck he saw people belting toward him. He had a feeling that his broken arm was back on square one. Yolanda Entallador landed first, raven hair swinging over her forehead as she touched ground. She held his head, crooning in Español. "I don't know what you're saying," he said with a smile, "but I love the way you say it." Then he fainted.

In the command post Lewis and Entallador hunched over the map.

"Han over the mountains headed north," an aide said, and placed half a dozen red pins in the map. "Blue sixteen has them sighted and requests orders."

Major Lewis looked up as Holcomb, the slender Peruvian girl at his side, stepped into the room. "They must have bred you for luck," he rasped. "Glad to see you're alive again. Have you any words of wisdom?"

"I beg your pardon, sir?".

"You got away with it but I don't know as I

could advise all my pilots to start ramming Han."

Holcomb explained his discovery of the weakness in Han shielding.

"Now that is useful!" Lewis turned to the ultraphonist and spread the word to his ship commanders.

In a running fight the Americans had an enormous edge in speed and maneuverability. Now they had a tactic that could take advantage of that: attacking in teams, the first ship would throw enough metal to put a few dings in Han shielding. The second wave would immediately follow before there was any chance of retreat or repair. The Americans began to win. As any old soldier knows and even politicians sometimes suspect, this is nicer than losing.

Although Holcomb pestered him for a new flying assignment, the combined human forces commander merely shrugged. "Try waving your arms real hard," he finally snapped. "I've got one ship left and I'll give it to a pilot with all his parts working. Relax for an hour. Entallador, this lot's getting close to your third jungle detachment. Can you hit them at that range?"

"Sí, mayor, fácilmente." The boss turned to give orders.

A hundred miles away the rockets lifted. Iron began to fly among the Han, doing their armor slight damage. The rockets were flashless and their crews presumably undetectable. But the Han began sweeping the jungle floor with dis when the barrage continued.

"How close are our ships?" Major Lewis asked.

"Within strike range, altitude ten thousand meters," the ultraphonist reported.

Lewis studied the screen which gave him a view of the maneuvering Han fleet from a scout floating high above the battlefield. "Señor Entallador, have yours give them one more round apiece and then scatter. The Han are zeroing in." He turned to the ultraphonist. "Strike force to start their dive as soon as the barrage lets up. How many ships has he?"

"Four, sir."

"Not enough. Tell him to concentrate on two enemy ships. If they live through that they can go to work on two more."

"Aye, sir."

The rocket attack ended and a few gunners were seen belting over treetops as they fled. The flashing blue *dis* rays of the Han opened great swaths of jungle, killing men almost as an unseen side effect of the process, but killing them very dead nonetheless.

"Where are those ships?" The major's teeth were clenched.

"Here they come sir." Fastmoving dots appeared on the left of the scope. *Dis* flashed as Americans closed with Han. One torpedo-shaped vessel staggered on its *rep* rays and went down. A cheer broke out in the command room. As rocket ships roared past the slower *rep*-propelled enemy, another beam holed a Han ship which thereupon wrecked itself with a series of explosions. The Han settled upright on the greenery below. Immediately Peruvians in dark green approached and attacked the stranded ship.

The American rockets were miles away over the mountains, just beginning their turn for the second run, when Peruvians resumed surface-to-air fire on the remaining Han ships and the Han slashed back with *dis*.

Meanwhile the crew—or robot, if there was no crew—in the grounded Han raider got a *dis* ray beaming from the ship's nose and a wide patch of jungle and a dozen men disappeared. Entallador groaned.

"Pull your men back," Lewis urged. "I'll get the strike groups to ray that bastard."

"*¡Absolutamente no! Este es un negocio para hombres.*" On the screen Lewis could see the *hombres* tending to their business.

Meanwhile, the other Han ships changed course and began climbing. American rockets buzzed past them and turned for another run. As they closed the Han released a pair of dark projectiles.

"Drop ships!" Major Lewis cried. The attacking rocket ships dodged the tiny vehicles, greeting them with a futile bombardment of explosives. One swerved in an attempt to ram the American. The other plunged earthward, ignoring fire and *dis*.

"It's going for the troops! Warn those—" The order to the Peruvians was too late. The missile struck—but not at the humans: it crashed into the grounded Han ship. The resulting explosion sent belting Peruvians away from ground zero much faster than they had intended to move.

"Hit his own ship by mistake!" Holcomb gasped.

"No mistake," Lewis said. "Señor Entallador, get your men in there to sift the wreckage. There's something there they don't want us to know about, or at least there was."

The Peruvian commander thought so too.

"What's the score?" Lewis asked.

"They flew off scope, sir," a tech replied. "Blue Sixteen is in pursuit but has inflicted no more casualities."

"Keep after them. Where's the Rathole gang now?"

"Captain Norris reports he's found another tunnel, sir."

The screen flickered for a moment, then the ultrascope stabilized. The American ship on tunnel detail, dis ray fixed in its nose, floated 300 meters above the jungle floor with its nose down like a browsing fish, blue dis ray boring into the earth below.

"He sure stirred up a response from the Han," the group commander said. "My compliments to the captain and tell him to probe west and south, try to pick up the continuation of his tunnel. Señor Entallador, can you get some ground support in there if those devils come out of their holes?"

"Yes, but my men must belt many leagues. If we had a ship—"

"I'll go," Holcomb offered hopefully, but his superior merely waved him to silence.

While the rocket ship continued to bore into the Han tunnels a scout reported a possible landing site for enemy ships in the nearby mountains. "Looks like a cave mouth," the observer phoned. "But ultrascope shows the whole area shielded. I can't make out details but the installation covers most of the mountain top."

"Blast!" Lewis looked at his map. "I've got more targets than ships. Tell that scout to main-

tain altitude and keep watching. Nasho, get
Niagra on the scrambler. I'll see if high command
can't shake loose another squadron."

The appeal was futile. The North American
command was maintaining hemisphere alert and
would not reassign ships to the actual war zone.
"I'll bet those pilots doing convoy duty in the
Rockies would love to buzz down here and get in
some shooting," Holcomb commented. The command was divided on policy but, for the moment
at least, the conservatives were running the show.
An appeal for Rogers brought only the news that
their champion had disappeared.

Ruth Harris burst into tears. "Tony, I can't believe it!" Rogers wondered what was the secret of
his fascination for the women of the Deering Clan.
First Wilma. . . . He gently disentangled himself
from Ruth's clutch. Harris quickly regained her
composure, watching his face for rejection.
Surely he had felt her attraction to him before his
transformation. But men were so dense.

"Still can't believe it myself," he grinned.
"Wolsky thinks he's solved the problem of my
suspended animation, and I suppose he has in a
way. The real problem is, who built the rejuvenation chamber—and why? Where are they now?

"Sit down," she urged. "Let me look at you.
You're just like you were when I was a little girl.
Maybe more handsome." She laughed. "I'm so
glad to see you alive."

Part of Ruth's case of nerves stemmed from her
sense of vulnerability: What would come of this
unnatrual combination of youth's uncontrollable
passion without youth's idealism—passion gov-

erned only by the hardwon cynicism of a lifetime?

He grinned. "The first time I popped into this world it seemed like a dream. It took years to stop thinking I'd go to sleep some night and wake up in 1927. Now I'm going through it all over again."

"Does it bother you?"

"I keep wondering—why me? I'm just an ordinary guy . . ."

"Tony Rogers," she laughed, "don't play modest; it's too absurd. You're not ordinary. You came out of the past to lead your country—the human race—to victory. Without you we would all still be Han slaves or hiding like hunted animals.

"Oh, come off it, Ruth," replied the hero. "The gangs were hardly wild animals. They had rockets, jump belts, inertron shielding."

"And they never mounted a campaign against their conquerors! They were too busy killing each other. You organized them."

"Where do we stand with the Han right now? I'd better go find out."

"Tony," She touched his arm. "you said a moment ago it was all a dream."

He put his hands on her shoulders. "Can you imagine it? Strength in my arms, wind on my face, the sun bright in my eyes again? To feel life's juices flow!"

For a repressed, forty year old spinster of Wilma's clan the memories were closer to home. Her pupils dilated as desire fused with fear. Now he was younger than she. If she let him escape, would she ever have another chance? "Door's locked." She had intended a seductive whisper but her voice cracked.

"Been a while," Rogers murmured, "but it's like a bicycle."

"What's a bicycle?"

"Something you ride. Once you've learned, you never forget how."

They pedalled furiously.

Twenty four hours later she saw him again: seething with repressed energy, unable to sit, pacing her office with clenched fists.

"Relax," she urged. "You said the Peruvians were doing fine. What's wrong? You just want to be down there in the thick of things, don't you?"

He laughed. "I guess that's part of it. But the HQ gang wants to keep my metamorphosis secret for a while, so I can't. But Lewis needs more men and ships and those generals are afraid to risk the fleet. 'What if a new pocket of underground Han appears?' they ask."

"You'd gamble, wouldn't you?"

"You're damned right I would. You don't win wars by sitting around in a funk waiting for the enemy. Besides, Holcomb's down there in sick bay. Entallador's daughter and he are—"

"Tony, if your friends are in danger, surely you can persuade the military—"

"I haven't been able to."

"General Gordon is a friend of yours."

"It's not so much him as Kindross and Maxi and others who run things now." Rogers was bitter.

"Kindross owes my clan. Let's see what I can do on the ultraphone."

Rogers suddenly remembered he had come originally to persuade this woman to a more aggressive policy because of her connections. He wondered how much of his persuasion was cerebral and how much by more elemental methods. "I'll be grateful for anything you try to do."

"I'll do it right now." She hesitated. "Tony, it would be better if Kindross didn't see you standing in the background."

He suspected that she also knew what would soon happen again if the charge kept building in this room and they brushed each other again. He left the building.

He was in a constant near-frenzy of arousal. Sexuality was one aspect, but there was also exuberant young muscle that shrieked for movement; in the two days since he had come out of stasis he had not slept. After he had endured hours of inactivity under Wolsky's instruments he mutinied and played jumpbelt football until Wolsky's students had collapsed. Then he had belted fifty odd miles to a rocket base for a hitch back to Niagra.

A rocket ship arrived after hasty conferences with Wolsky and Ruth Harris opened the possibility that young Rogers was not an absurd impostor. After an unsatisfactory interview with General Gordon in Niagra he had eaten a huge meal and, having nothing else to do, had wangled a scout rocket and gone back to Ruth for an encounter which had left her in a state of dreamy satiation and Rogers with the feeling that he had just consumed a Chinese dinner. Hungry as ever, he had then flown back to Niagra and another briefing.

I've got to get this under control, he resolved as he pulled on his jump belt and hurtled over the college. He continued his internal monologue as he tarzaned from tree to tree.

What would your average eighty three year old man do if he was suddenly twenty five again? The same thing Rogers felt like doing every twenty minutes! How long since any daydream of goatish conquest had not been spoiled by the memory of Wilma's fiercely possessive monogamy? Was he using Ruth, or was it deeper than that? The image that rose irresistibly was of a slender darkhaired form, accompanied by the musky scent of the scarf that was still tucked in his pocket. If Ngo-Lan was still alive and he was young . . . and Wilma was . . . He pulled himself together and tried to think about the military situation in Peru.

Major Lewis was in a tight spot. Norris's probes seemed close to a Han strongpoint. Ground troops sallied into the valley. At the same time Han airships were sighted near Puerto Nateles. Lewis did not have the ships to cover both areas. Secure in their Niagra bunker, HQ was sending pious utterances about making-do when they should have been sending help.

Entallador's troops were making forced march to the new outbreak but it might take days to reach the remote cañons where the American underground assault team was in business. The battle with the Han fleet had left him an air force of four ships and two scouts. The Han, his pilots swore, had all been blown out of the sky.

Down in the Rathole the enemy melted away as Americans used probe holes to drop behind them into Han tunnels. But an advance unit had no sooner discovered a new tunnel under Mount Apolillado farther south when the whole side of the peak exploded. Devastation spread down the valley. Radiation detectors aboard circling ships pegged their needles.

Lewis chanted words learned from boys his mother had warned him not to play with. A third of his ground force was gone. Han soldiers in rad armor erupted from the demolished mountain and swept down, beaming *dis* on his surviving troops. "Get ships in there before they're overrun!" he bellowed.

Two ships got close enough to support the demoralized soldiers with heavy rockets. The Han faltered and there was time for the dismayed Americans to see there were only a few dozen of them. Rocket shells began to take their toll. The Americans got back onto their feet and advanced.

Then Han airships struck. There were only five but Lewis's two ships were caught close to the ground, one slammed into the earth by a combined *dis* and *rep* ray attack while the other escaped into the sky and hovered to study the odds. They were not good.

The vidscreen shook. "Commander," the spy craft pilot said, "permission to attack?"

"Stay aloft! Get me Blue Six. Tell him to drop any present business and get flitting. Where are Entallador's people?"

The picture tore and dissolved, to be replaced by a slim yellow face with gray eyes.

"—desperate attack on the Han Empire by human forces under the barbarous Anthony Rogers thrown back by my loyal troops. Know then, beasts of Earth: Prince Mordred has other bases. The sleeping armies of Han are yet to be awakened. The doom of the murderous human race is sealed. I go now to rouse the hidden armies that will destroy you with one fell swoop."

"Get a fix on that transmitter!" Lewis snapped. "And get Niagra no matter what their excuse is. Do we have a scout? Holcomb, get that busted sled of yours airborne. We'll track that silky serpent to his hole!"

"Yes sir!" Holcomb and his lovely companion raced for the door.

"The legions of the master race shall march again," the image continued, "trampling the dirtborn spawn of this miserable planet back into the mire which nurtured them." The image began to fade.

"Sounds just like he knew some other better planet," a human voice observed with amusement.

"Stratospheric, Major," a technician said. "Very high and moving south."

"Get Holcomb on it. We can't spare anybody else." The screen went blank. "Where's our scout ship? Who's in contact with Norris?"

"Situation at Mt. Apolillado unchanged, Major," said an aide. "The Han made one pass and turned south."

"Get me a projection on their course. Try for an intercept with Blue Six."

The Peruvian girl had already lost one husband. She pressed a hand to her breast and then undid the front of Holcomb's blouse to place her warm hand over his heart. "Mi cielo, te van a matar," she mourned.

"I'll be careful." He held her with his good arm, then turned to climb into the one man scout—a canopied sled. He waved, then concentrated on onehanded flying. The scout rose slowly.

"Get me a fix, Blue Central," he called.

"Ninety eight degree azimuth from you, heading south at fourteen thousand meters."

At that altitude Holcomb would be able to squeeze more speed out of the sled but he would have about as much maneuverability as a bullet. "Got an image?"

"He's shielded and he's quit transmitting."

"That's just dandy. Got any more helpful news?"

"The Han that attacked Blue Twelve are headed your way."

"I'll be too high and fast by the time they get here. Try to keep a trace on the guy I'm chasing. And give me a course prediction."

"Aknol. Will do."

Holcomb gave his tiny ship full power. Moments later the HQ tech called, "We have course prediction and an intercept vector."

"Intercept? I can't see a thing and the sky's clear."

"You're looking the wrong way. The Han are on your tail."

"Where is he?" Rogers demanded.

"Chasing a Han ship, Marshal." The comtech couldn't believe this youth wasn't an impostor, no matter what his crew boss said.

"But he can't fly. He's injured!"

"I'm just giving you the report from Peru."

Must really be short of pilots, Rogers thought. What could force Lewis to send out a wounded pilot on a job like that? Any number of things, he had to admit. He grunted an "Aknol," and snapped off. He had to get to Niagra fast.

Rogers took off before he could become enmeshed in the laborious process of thinking things out. Ah, thoughtless youth! Niagara cleared and he poured on the power. He tuned his ultraphone to command frequency and after thirty minutes of dial twisting finally achieved a lock-in with the Puerto Nateles channel. He listened in disbelief.

The ultrascope trace had disappeared while moving south. Holcomb and two rocket ships had engaged in a brief dogfight with the escaping Han. One American had been grounded and the other had gone to pick him up. High above the Pacific's clouds Holcomb saw the surviving Han pass beneath. He took up pursuit.

"Holcomb!" Rogers broke in on the command frequency without IDing. "Watch it. That's a trap!"

"Who are you?" Blue Central demanded. "Give location and code."

"This is Rogers, Marshal Rogers, blast it! I'm still over Texas. I don't know what my number is. I'm not supposed to be on this channel."

"Tony, is that really you?" Holcomb asked.

"Does Señor Entallador's recently widowed daughter-in-law have long black hair?"

"She'll not have it when we're finished with her!" a Han voice snarled.

"It's him, Jake," Holcomb said. "What are you up to now, Marshal?"

"My god, they're picking up ultraphone!" somebody howled.

"No they're not. Some equine anus left that

radio on. We're rebroadcasting everything!"

"Sweet mother!"

"Holcomb, keep tuned to me," Rogers said. "There may be other ships besides the one you're chasing."

"Aknol, sir. I'm boring in."

Rogers keyed his phone to keep the circuit open and changed frequency. In a minute he had a military relay in Niagra. "Get me Dr. Harris at the University," he instructed.

The ship's only vidplate was connected to the probe but Ruth's voice was cheerful. She sobered when Rogers answered her questions.

"Tony, what are you doing out there? You've got no business tearing off on your own."

"Doc, I know my trade. I called to ask you for help."

She sighed. "Tell me what you need."

"Pressure on General Gordon and the staff. More ships down here."

"I'll try. Tony, can I tell them where you are, what you're doing?"

"Better not. On their books I'm still eighty three. They'll order me back to Niagra. They can't make me but I don't need arguments right now and I may need their cooperation later."

"I'll have to tell them I talked with you."

"But you don't know where I am. They'll guess but I won't check in at Puerto Nateles so officially I'll not be under any command."

"Tony, be careful."

"Thanks for helping. I knew you would."

Of course you did, she thought. You can't be as naive as you pretend. Maybe I'm the ingenue.

"Uncle Chax," she was saying a half hour later,

"national prestige be damned! The Deering clan builds rocket motors. The present situation calls for worldwide deployment. I'm not even considering the losses to enemy action—and we've taken losses. Of course I'm sure. I've been talking to Rogers.Now there must be some hawks on the council. They'll need your help to send an expeditionary force into Peru."

"I won't throw in with Dupre's crowd. If you think—"

Dr. Harris sighed. "Uncle Chax, you employ a lot of metal techs in that Nevada inertron plant. They're highly skilled. Would you care to guess who trained them?"

The man stared at his vidplate. "You—"

"Uncle, I was seven the last time you won any game of skill from me. Now this Peruvian business is important. It will also do the clan no damage to land on the right side for once."

"All right, lady. I aknol." Like Rogers, Uncle Chax had married into the clan. Like Rogers he respected the men and enjoyed their company. But those Deering women . . .

Ruth slumped. Her palms were damp. She thought she hated doing that sort of thing. Now to call Rink at the Nevada plant and warn him. Then call Tony back. Then . . .

The tiny scout ship flashed over the ocean. Below him Holcomb saw three Han cruisers plodding south on rep rays, apparently oblivious to the American's stratospheric passage. There was nothing ahead but ice—he thought. And where was that high-flying Han ship? His beam swept the sky.

When solid ice appeared on the scope he was groggy from lack of sleep, but he discovered that his quarry now occasionally flickered on the scope. Masses of gray cloud blanketed any landmark; he had to call Puerto Nateles and ask for a triangulation on his signal to determine his location. As night fell the cloud mass rose until even at his altitude the stars were hidden, but the ultrascope beam held his target. Despite increasing turbulence he forged on in the wake of his quarry.

High over Central America Rogers' fast scout rode the upper edge of the atmosphere. The sinking sun caught the underside of his stubbywinged craft, turning it bright gold despite the camouflage paint Americans still used on all their war craft.

Though by now everyone knew Rogers was aloft and trailing Holcomb by a quarter of a planet, Niagra remained mute. He cursed chain-of-command and wished for the old days when a boss made instant decisions.

Dawn brought no relief to Holcomb's little ship pushing through dense antarctic clouds. One of the Han slipped off his scope. Plunging deeper into the storm, he found his quarry, sledding on the ice. He left it and followed the second after dropping an ultrabeam target which the wind carried wide of the downed Han.

The second Han began a wide spiral slowed and buffeted by surface winds. Keeping station with the sled became increasingly difficult. Beyond the ultron canopy he could eyeball nothing but snow, but the ultrascope showed the cigarlike Han ship and a stark outcropping of rock through the ice cap, while the ice itself was distorted into wild crags and pressure ridges that seemed to move even as he watched. He wondered if the downed ship had been damaged by the storm. When he reported to Puerto Nateles and Rogers both urged him to abandon the pursuit.

"I can hold on," Holcomb answered. "This second crawler is looking for something. I'll stick until I find—" Engaged in a three way conversation, Holcomb was unprepared for the drop ship that flashed past. *Dis* bathed him, dispersing weather to leave him in vacuum until the projectile-like vessel had passed beneath him. The storm closed in again with a thunderclap.

"Wow!" He dived after the crop ship. Close to the surface, the larger Han craft bathed the sky with *dis*.

"Get the hell out of there!" Rogers called. "You're outgunned."

"*Marshal Rogers?*" A new voice came on channel. Rogers had no screen but that unemotional voice sent a chill through him. There was no accent he could identify. The timbre made it surely male.

"Who are you?"

"Prince Mordred, you genocidal maniac. Are you in that flitter? You insult me with a chase too easy."

"Sorry to disappoint you, prince," Holcomb interrupted. "Marshal Rogers is thousands of kilometers away—and you haven't trapped anyone yet." He punctuated his reply with a rocket. The explosive left a faint smudge on the Han cruiser. Holcomb swore.

"Between the fury of the elements and the fury of the master race you are powerless."

"Mordred," Tony said, "the War of Liberation is over. I can offer you and any surviving Han leniency if you surrender immediately."

"Anyone can offer," the Han said drily. "But can even the great Rogers deliver? In any event, I seek no quarter nor do I offer any. Extermination was what you always proposed. While you did not annoy us we Han let you grub in the forest. Enslavement! With Han machines what need have we of unsanitary humans? A lifetime ago you repaid our forebearance with extermination. I rejoice that you have lived so long. Now you shall learn the meaning of the word."

"The radio is off," a faint voice protested. "He's using ultraphone!"

Why had the military never devised codes for the inevitable day when their enemies would penetrate their comm networks? There was no way for Rogers to get an uncompromised message to Holcomb or Niagra. He rotated the loop and hurriedly noted azimuths. "Holcomb," he said, "come on out of there. We've got a fix. The fleet can take it from here."

No answer. Rogers repeated his message.

No reply.

"Niagra?"

"Here, sir."

"Get a fix on me. Have you got one on the Han transmitter?"

"Aknol. Coordinates are—" He rattled off the numbers. "Your present fix, sir," began the tech at Niagra.

"Whose side are you on?" Rogers snarled.

"Aknol. Carrier wave from Blue Thirteen has stopped. Frequency of Puerto Nateles is two twenty eight point six, for Everglades Beacon is fourteen oh seven point nine, for MexTex Tower is—" He continued with a string of numbers and ground station locations.

"The Han will be delighted to know that," Rogers said acidly but the voice droned on oblivious. "Ground beacon blue twenty six is eight two sixteen and one half. Brazillo Rocket Port is nine nineteen twenty point three—"

Tony let him drone on as he noted the frequency of the locator the broadcaster had slipped him. When the transmission ended he merely said, "Aknol Blue One. What name, friend?"

"Jerina, sir."

"Thanks. Beam off." So they were not total idiots at Niagra . . .

Tony tuned the locator. The signal was faint and overlain with atmospherics from what must be a most ungodly storm. Even if the Han hadn't got him, Holcomb wouldn't last long on the ground in such conditions.

It took full power to progress into the storm. The beam he followed was feeble; Rogers had to keep close to the surface, where winds tore still more desperately at his little ship. American science could make a ship weightless but do nothing about mass or inertia. He nosed into driving snow probing constantly.

He picked up the Han crusier now half buried in snow. He had assumed the fallen ship was bait to trap Holcomb but perhaps the vessel really was damaged. The young lieutenant shouldn't be far from here. He tried the ultraphone again.

Nosing into the wind, Rogers brought his scout

over the stranded enemy. Instantly dis lanced out
to bathe his inertron shielding. The scout lunged
ahead, momentarily free of the wind, then
slammed to a halt as the projector went off. Rogers
held his fire. His tiny rocket guns were surely
useless unless he was lucky enough to put a ding
in Han armor and follow through with dis. The
weather did not encourage this maneuver.

Kilometers away the ultrabeam picked out a
giant ice chasm. Invisible in the storm, Rogers
inched over it, probing for bottom. Thousands of
meters below the continental rock was bare. He
hovered, searching for any sign of humanity.

The tiny craft was buffeted by the wind as he
flew onehanded, constantly refocusing the scope
with the other. Headed into the storm he could
either creep or, by reducing throttle slightly,
move backward. What he could not do was re-
verse course: to turn downwind this close to the
ground was premeditated suicide.

Persistence paid off when he came upon metal
buried in the snow beyond the chasm. He narrowed the focus and brought in a view of an
ultron-canopy. Holcomb was gone.

Whatever had induced him to leave? Rogers
crept closer, wondering how he would anchor the
weightless scout long enough to look around. Finally he drove it under the snow as Holcomb must
have. No longer buffeted by the storm, he probed
methodically and finally saw Holcomb huddled
in an ice cave.

Through ice the beam did not give enough detail to see if Holcomb was breathing. Rogers
zipped his jacket and found the stratosphere
breathing mask. It would protect his face. He

tightened the strap on his helmet, pulled ultra-phone ear flaps down, and lowered his goggles.

The ship carried gear for high altitude bailouts and a fair amount of it was adaptable to this cold. He found gloves, a first aid kit, food and water rations. Rogers chewed gorp and hung the rest of the kit on his belt. He had yet to adjust to his new body's constant demands for food.

Cabin search yielded a hand dis gun, which he attached to his belt, leaving his rocket pistol in its usual position. He considered taking off his belt; weight might be an advantage against the storm. But even though a jump in this wind might take him to New Zealand, long habit made Rogers keep the belt on.

Wind and snow tore as he opened the ultron canopy. He got his bearings and crawled, count-ing meters. Near the ice cave he set the hand dis at lowest power and began melting holes. Almost immediately he located a tunnel blocked with soft snow. He cleared the passage. Next to the uncon-scious Holcomb was a cold survival-kit alcohol stove.

"Oxygen gone," Rogers grunted. He held his breath and dissed a vent in the cave roof. Holcomb mumbled as Rogers rummaged the medkit for a stimulant.

"Who?"

"Tony Rogers."

Painfully, Holcomb tried to focus. "Can't be."

"I've been taking vitamins. Can you walk?"

"Took a hit. Luck ran out."

"Your luck will never run out. I've got a ship."

Rogers wondered if he could ever lift off in this storm. Holcomb tried to stand, which convinced

Rogers that he would have to be carried. He slung the pilot over his back and began crawling back to his ship.

Then the ice shook—an ominous vibration, as if the continent were splitting apart.

Rogers had little choice but to continue crawling until he reached the new chasm. The far side was invisible in the murk. Of his rocket ship there was no trace.

VII

Rogers dissed a trench and left Holcomb in it. He could not see the bottom of the new chasm. His only hope lay in returning to Holcomb's downed flyer. He hoisted him again and crept through windswept dunes of snow. With dis he exposed the disabled ship, stowed the wounded man, comatose again, and examined it. Part of one control surface had been dissed. It would not fly. If the weather calmed it might float. When would that be?

The ultraphone was dead but the scope still worked. Rogers whistled through his teeth as he swept the area. The chasm to the north had been two kilometers long and half a kilometer across at its widest. His ship had not fallen in. It rested on a precarious isthmus of ice!

The only approach was around the end of the crevasse. Beyond, near the Han ship, were figures in bulky weather suits, and pieces of equipment. His continued sweep picked up metal coming from the south. He adjusted focus and it was a squat, streamlined tractor a hundred meters long crawling rapidly through the ice, leveling pressure ridges with a turret-mounted dis ray. The vehicle was heading toward him. Another sweep revealed no more surprises. Rogers searched the flyer for rations. He aroused Holcomb and made him eat, then devoured the rest himself. He found a battery and shells for the rocket pistol. "Time to move," he said, and opened the canopy.

He could not use his jump belt, but he had to move somehow, so Rogers stripped it off to give his body weight and he lashed his extra equipment to the floating belt and tethered it with a strap to his waist. He ballasted Holcomb with a cockpit seat to keep him from blowing away, buttoned up as best he could, and proceeded to circumnavigate the chasm dragging, perforce, Holcomb and his equipment behind him.

Back in the Wyoming Valley, General Gordon had asked Dr. Wolsky for a briefing and tour of the fantastic chamber down in the old coal mine. The little scientist responded with mixed feelings. While Wolsky had no time to explain things to people who lacked the necessary technical background, Gordon represented a conduit between Wolsky and grant money. The faucet could turn either way.

With careful discavation the original chamber had been made the center of a larger vault. It had been learned that the original chamber was only one of several bubbleshaped structures, all of which were shielded and all of whose functions remained hazy. One was probably a power supply for shields and equipment. What had triggered the device was still a mystery.

Gordon sat in an office in a temporary building

erected to replace a tent that had once collapsed on Wolsky. Wolsky thought the tour was about to begin, and was warming up with a lecture.

"Put a rat in the chamber—nothing," Wolsky said. "A dead rat—nothing. Dying rat—still nothing. Yet something triggers the chamber to come to the aid of a dead or dying Rogers twice in five hundred years."

"Rats!" The general's remark was more expletive than comment. "Why rats? The machine is designed to treat a man."

"Any man? First five centuries, then three days. I cannot ask for volunteers. Next we try monkeys and—"

"No monkey business!" The general leaned across the table. Behind, his bodyguard shifted uneasily. "You're going to put me in next, Doctor."

"No!" Wolsky said. "Do you suppose I have not thought of going myself? No one who sees Rogers in his new body—But maybe it only takes Rogers. Or maybe next time it will again take five centuries."

"I'm not asking you and I'm not going to argue," Gordon said. "As a favor, you can take samples before we start."

Wolsky glanced skyward but there was no answer there.

"Or I can save you some time by letting you read this." Gordon handed the scientist an envelope. Wolsky opened it and the first paper was headed "Biopsy report." He pushed it back into the envelope.

"I'm sorry," Wolsky said.

"Why? I've had a good life. I just happen to be

greedy enough to want a little more."

An hour later the general lay down on the table that had accepted Rogers. A technician looked up from his scope. "We've got power flow!"

The force screen was abruptly there, separating the adamant general from the rest of the world—even from his bodyguard. Wolsky faced them and shrugged. "Now we wait."

Entallador had spent an exhausting night in conference with his lieutenants, both in person and by ultraphone. Now his wounded *guerrilleros* were beginning to arrive. He was in no mood to listen to complaints from an old fisherman but he knew his duty. "Come along," he said.

The fishermen were a factor Entallador could not ignore in this port's economy. He walked down the narrow street to the harbor. The question seemed to be something about docking rights. Why did they need him to adjudicate?

When he neared *la esplanada* he could see the problem. The docks had disappeared. Waves were knocking down houses a block inland. "Where do you wish to dock now?" Entallador asked.

The fisherman looked unhappy. "Over here on Portolá Road, señor boss, but the Señora Vellaes objects to ships in her yard and the smell of fish on her front porch."

The wind had abated somewhat. Rogers' gloves protected his hands from jagged ice but not from the cold. Within a couple of hundred meters the knees of his uniform had worn through and he was leaving pink tracks in the snow, so he ripped strips from his jacket lining and bound them around his knees. He tried belting for short stretches, skimming the surface and outwaiting gusts, but he kept ramming into ragged ice outcrops and soon gave up. He labored in a howling twilight where visibility was arm's length at best, and often less. The ear pieces of his ultraphone protected him from the wind's roar but also kept out all other sound. Deafened, blinded, he crawled.

Far ahead the enemy tractor halted. Rays flared and ice became steam, exposing the grounded Han ship. Workers in bulky suits climbed over the wreck, covering it with a tough transparent canopy which they inflated. Inside, men belted about spraying hardening-catalyst.

The tractor captain grunted as his scope revealed an unexpected mass of metal. Soon he knew it was a ship. It seemed abandoned. Without clearing with Command, he buzzed two units out from under the weather canopy.

Rogers crawled five hours before he rounded the end of the new chasm. Leaving Holcomb in a hollow, he crept to the edge. The ice was smooth and slippery. Visibility was better now but he could still not see bottom. He thought he could hear the gurgle of water. Ice melting? Probably he was hearing avalanches. He crawled back. Holcomb had regained consciousness. "I can't believe it's you, sir."

"I can hardly believe it myself."

"Let me rest a moment and I'll try to walk."

"Nobody can walk in this," Rogers said. "Get on my back."

An hour later as they drank melted snow and

scraped ice off their unifroms Holcomb complained, "Couldn't you at least have chosen the scenic route?"

There was a rumble. The ice shook like the skin of a horse trying to shake off a fly. "Not scenic," Rogers said, "but exciting."

"How far?"

"Close, I think." Rogers wished the visibility would improve. He crawled up over a pressure ridge. "Ah," he said. "There's the ship."

The stubby fish shape was wedged into the crevasse. Rogers was dissing the thick coating of ice away when somewhere above them sounded a wail higher pitched than the wind. He slid back the canopy and helped Holcomb into a seat. With a canopy lowered they were out of the storm at last. "Cold," Holcomb muttered.

"I'll get the heater going. But first let's lift: there's something funny going on out there." Rogers peeled gloves from numb hands, fumbled at the controls and prayed nothing else would go wrong.

Whap! A scarlet line struck the transparent ultron over their heads and adhered like the tentacle of some sea monster.

"Where'd that come from?" Rogers snarled.

Holcomb looked back. "It's taut all the way back up. Give it a tug with the motors."

"We're moving."

"Somebody's coming down that line toward us. I'll open the canopy and try dissing him."

"Don't!" Two could play that game—Rogers' warning was punctuated by a blast of dis which bathed the ship with pale blue luminescence. "I'd better get us airborne before we have unwelcome company."

The maneuver was not that easy. The chasm was narrow and twisting. Roger crept the ship forward.

"Getting closer," Holcomb said. "Let me try a shot."

"That's what he wants you to do. You'll take us both to zero," Rogers said. "I'm heading topside now. Get the scope going and try to see where he came from. He won't be alone." He nosed up and shot out into the storm. Instantly the wind seized the rocket ship and swept it away across the ice.

"Hold her head," Holcomb cried. "I'm trying to get a fix on the Han."

"I'm trying." Rogers risked a quick look over his shoulder: far from having been swept away, the enemy in his bulky suit was not just hanging on; he was methodically creeping up the line! Rogers grunted.

"Something parked next to the Han ship," Holcomb reported. "but I can't focus in tightly enough."

"Don't try. Sweep a full circle. Open up the HQ phone. With that guy on our tail and reporting our position it's no use pretending there ain't nobody here but us chickens."

"Doesn't seem to be anything airborne."

"Downwind? I want to get out of here fast."

The icy blast whirled the weightless ship and tossed it south. The thin red line cracked like a whip, but the heavily suited figure held—and kept inching closer.

"More men belting this way," Holcomb reported. "Oops! They're being scattered by the wind."

Rogers strove for altitude. "Sweep ahead for mountains quick. And think up some way to dump our hitchhiker. He's holding us down."

Holcomb had never heard of a hitchhiker. "If you mean the guy on the rope, I can go out on the hull with a knife. You've got flat terrain for a hundred kilometers as far as I can see."

"Let's see if I can flip him."

"Tony, I don't think this guy is a Han. That last snap would have broken my back if I'd been out there. He just quits crawling and hangs on."

"Wish I knew what that line was made of. Hey—incoming!" Bright-yellow flared in front of them, dispersing clouds and shaking the little ship.

"Guy on our rear got hit!" Holcomb yelled.

"Han!" Rogers growled. "Don't even respect their own lives."

The next explosion was farther away and to the rear.

"You wouldn't know this," Rogers said. "but back at Belleau Wood that would be a bracketing shot. The next salvo is going to come right where we'd better not be." He dived for the ice. Below, another crevasse opened invitingly. The first round exploded above. Bits of steel rattled off the ship's inertron body. The second round spun the ship and carried Rogers off course.

"Guy on the rope's catching hell."

"So are we." Rogers found the crevasse on the scope and hurtled down, hardly slowing until walls of green were inches away as the ship spun and weaved through the ice. "And now maybe we lose him," Rogers said. Ahead the ice closed in to less than a meter, then widened briefly. He swung the ship up, out—and immediately back into the crevasse. The slender scarlet line slipped through the impasse. The implacable armored figure snagged. The line held and the ship shook as if it had taken a hit. Then the tentacle peeled from the ultron canopy with a sound like a string of fire-crackers.

Rogers nosed up out of the chasm and hedgehopped the ice fields only meters from the surface. He worried about that Han had scraped loose. That tough stranger might still be alive.

Antarctica is 4000 kilometers across. Its ice cap averages two kilometers deep. Twelve thousand or so cubic kilometers of ice or, in terms Rogers found more familiar, three thousand cubic miles of ice. Every one of them was melting.

"My orders are to report to you, Major Lewis, but also to dispatch scouts farther south to inves-tigate enemy activity, and to extend the search for Marshal Rogers. You are to brief me on details." The trim air officer in gray remained at attention, helmet under his arm.

"Relax. Sit down if you can find a place." Lewis was haggard and unshaven. Across the room the big situation map covered a five-by-four meter light table over which two Peruvians were bent, faces shining in its light. Two walls were lined with vid screens, before each of which sat or stood an American with earphones and chest mike. The newcomer scanned the room with a practiced eye. Many screens showed empty sky, but on one troops stalked cautiously past a tunnel intersection and on another lightly clad humans crawled over a downed Han ship. One plate showed the town outside, the ocean now halfway up to the plaza: the new beach was littered with uprooted trees and those few parts of stone and mud houses that would float.

Lewis noticed his gaze. "We're evacuating in twenty four hours," he said. "Entallador's going to put us up in some caves in the mountains. Now, here's the situation . . ."

Blasting low over the iceberg littered sea, the scout ship strove to outrun the wind. Behind Rogers Holcomb dozed. All his instruments were in the red: power low, hull breached, airspeed unsafe, antigravs on overload, while beneath the ship ice floes ground and smashed. Suddenly three dots appeared on the screen. Rogers dived. The ultraphone crackled but his screens were up so he got only part of the message. "Blue Thirteen from Kappa Four." He was exhausted and hungry. His ship would probably not make it to South America anyway. He keyed the switch. "Blue Thirteen. Repeat message."

"All units deploy. ID please. Blue Thirteen, this is Kappa Four from Niagra. Drop your shield for an ultra beam scan."

"Drop yours if you're young and trusting." Rogers plunged closer to the ice-flecked sea. If the hull was intact he could duck underwater . . .

"This is Carson. Will, is that you?" Rogers' beam picked up a dark round face. Certainly didn't look like a Han!

"Holcomb's asleep. This Rogers." He replied without thinking.

"Drop your screens, Marshal. We've been looking for you."

Tony swept the ultrabeam across the other ship. It looked American.

"I said 'Cut your jets.' " The face on the screen grew grim. "Land on the nearest berg and climb out. One false move and you're zero."

"Don't strain your milk," Rogers said. "I can prove who I am."

"Sure. Just send me your prints over the ultrascope. I've got a whole lab here to analyze them." The American's voice changed. "That ship ain't Blue Thirteen!"

"Wake up Will, we're in trouble," Rogers urged, but his wounded pilot only grunted. Rocket shells burst like a steel hailstorm. "I was praying for help," Rogers snarled, "and when it shows up they shoot at me."

"Try another god next time," the scout said. "The last person you look like is Marshal Rogers."

"Get Niagra; they'll confirm." A second salvo knocked his ship into a roll. "I'm coming down. Hold your fire."

A large berg loomed. He limped in and hovered, nose to the wind. "Commander," Rogers asked, "where are you from?"

"None of your business! Where are you from?"

"From the past," Rogers said tiredly.

"What's your wife's name?"

"Wilma."

"Clan?"

"Deering." Rogers hesitated. This triggerhappy

dingbat—"Offhand, I'd say you were one of that fortunate lot."

"How would you know?" The pilot's voice deepened with suspicion."

"Certain family resemblances," Rogers said. "Now you tell me exactly how many degrees of consanguinity lie between me, yourself, and Dr. Ruth Harris."

"Where'd you ever hear of—"

"Now I know you're a Deering." Rogers paused. "It might profit you to know that Marshal Rogers is carrying a wounded companion. Not even Deering kin will save your skin once you've killed your supreme commander. Now Marshal Rogers is hungry, Marshal Rogers is tired, and Marshal Rogers is sorely tempted to abuse the authority of his position!"

"Come out of the ship with your hands up."

The technicians called Dr. Wolsky.

"Looks like the same pattern we saw with Rogers just before he emerged," he agreed. "If he gets out of the force field before I arrive, hold him below ground."

"How am I supposed to persuade the general's bodyguard?"

"To be a scientist requires daring and imagination."

It took hours for the small man to fly from the university; to his surprise General Gordon had not yet emerged when he arrived. Standing in the underground chamber, he checked the readings. "Looks good up to here," he pointed. "Has anyone touched the energy bubble?"

"Not a chance, Doctor. Not until you got here."

"Good, good. The ultra beam."

Seated behind a jury-rigged concrete screen only meters from the energy field, the scientist switched it on. The crowd in the chamber gasped. Wolsky stood to look over the top of the screen.

The field had collapsed at the first touch of the probe. Featureless pink tissue spilled across the floor. As they watched, it ruptured—unable to support its own weight. Blood trickled down the exposed surface like a vermilion spider web.

"Get a *dis* ray and zero that monstrosity!" somebody cried.

"Do not you dare!" Wolsky shrieked. He ran forward to stare. "Get me instruments!"

"Dr. Wolsky," an aide gasped, "What do you think happened?"

"It's hard to say, but if General Gordon could hear me I think he'd agree that the machine does not cure cancer."

"Even if this were a pure culture carcinoma," a student objected, "It would have long ago outgrown its blood supply. It should be necrotic."

"Very observant, but you see it bleed, you see it pulse. It has a circulatory system!"

"A giant cancer? My God, destroy it!"

"Idiot!" Wolsky cried. "The machine has created this thing from the substance of General Gordon. Think what we may learn! We must keep it alive!"

VIII

The Peruvians carefully worked their way up the side of the mountain in single file while above them floated anti-grav sleds and small bundles on jump belts, like a collection of misshapen balloons.

Major Lewis clumped along on foot. Behind him walked a young man of more than medium height clad in a fresh gray and blue uniform. "I still can't believe it, Marshal. If HQ says you have a foolproof ID we lesser mortals must accede. But the only way my mind can handle it is to think of you as a new person entirely."

"It's not all that easy for me." Rogers trod carefully along a ten-centimeter wide ledge with a thousand meter drop on his right. "My body is young again. It feels great. But my mind is still eighty three—when it's not playing at being fifteen."

"Hard to deal with, I suppose?"

Rogers laughed. "The appetites never go away. But suddenly I can do all the things I've only remembered."

"The appetites," Major Lewis mused.

Rogers laughed again. "I was thinking more of an appetite for action."

"You'll get more than you want before this is over," Lewis said.

Entallador had set up the command in a cave. The floor was wet and there was a constant drip of cold water from stalactites. A work detail was in the process of stretching plastic sheeting.

"I've had a day's rest," Rogers said. "Where can you use me best?"

"Talk to Entallador. He's in full command of the ground. I don't want to bump one of my pilots."

"How's my pilot doing?"

"Fine. We got a cargo ship down from MexTex to fly out the wounded."

"Héroe," the smitten Yolanda Entallador murmured. "Mi héroe."

"Sweetheart," Holcomb stroked her black hair. "I won't be gone long. Rogers will need me as soon as my arm's better. I'll come back." Holcomb knew no other airman was going to get assigned personal pilot to the Marshal, because Rogers now did his own flying. But still, with Rogers' friendship he should be able to get back to the front lines again even though it would mean forms and requests through Niagra.

He looked into Yolanda's eyes. He would manage the transfer somehow. He swore he would. He bent to kiss her.

Entallador gestured at his map. "The same problem always, Marshal. When I have men they have no equipment. When I have weapons, I do not have men. *Now* Niagra sends belts, rockets, *dis.* Now that half my people are dead."

Rogers tried to look sympathetic. Now that he was young again it was less easy. His eyes lit on diagrams of the underground city that the Andean boss had tossed aside. He persuaded Entallador to summarize the situation.

Two units of twenty men each still advanced through partly destroyed radioactive ruins. A smaller group followed the ships south through jungle, hunting their base. There, Rogers thought, was the likeliest place for Han survivors. Entallador, of course, wanted to root out all the Han. But Rogers knew there was a more serious threat somewhere in Antarctica.

Still, Rogers supposed, it would be best to finish this battle quickly and then go into Antarctica. He volunteered to transport the South American troops together with as much in the way of supplies as he could tow. Major Lewis agreed but put him in charge of ten Americans heading for the front by sled. Rogers accepted the assignment with mixed feelings. He wanted to reach the surviving Han before Ngo-Lan was captured and killed. But he was, after all, on this side of the war.

He reported to Señora Beliza and took command. The departing team turned their gear and rad armor over to the newcomers, and took the unloaded sled back to the Peruvian base. Rogers donned bulky rad armor with a built-in belt. He carried a portable *dis* projector and an infra red scope with flip up goggles on his helmet. He

checked the map, posted his command, and went
to inspect his probe teams.

The mountain had been honeycombed. Passages close to the surface had been slagged by
Prince Mordred's farewell blast. Teams had
probed these with dis holes, avoiding shielded
areas. Rogers skimmed just above the tunnel floor
searching in darkness with his infra red scope.

The men he joined, a big Northerner and a slender Peruvian, were Operation Rathole veterans.
They had a routine. One would set up the dis. The
other would go back fifty meters and take cover.
The dis ray man would lie flat and fire his beam.
When the dust settled the rear man would fly in
over him, rocket pistols ready. They had survived
more booby traps than any other assault group.

"Then let's not meddle with a winning system," Rogers said. "I'll just add myself to the team
and see how it works."

He sensed that these quietly competent men
were not eager for aid—not even from the eternal
Rogers.

"Fine," the American said. "But you'd better
stay in the rear until you get the hang of it."

"Cualquier descuido y este cabrón nos mata,"
the Peruvian growled.

"He's teaching me Español," Block said. "Do
you know what *cabrón* means?"

"He can teach me too if things get dull," Rogers
said. "Where's your next move?"

Block produced a grubby, hand drawn map.
"Here's where we are. There have been no Han, no
robot attacks for nearly a kilometer. Either this,"
he pointed, "is the end of the complex or there's

something down at the next level." He turned to fiddle with the ultrascope. "This penetrates rock for a depth of about five hundred meters and then loses resolution. It looks solid ahead, but we're going to blast a couple of test holes."

"Let me be the *dis* man; you two stay back and direct me for a while," Rogers volunteered. They nodded. Trailing the heavy projector on a floating frame, Rogers advanced. Han tunnels here seemed long abandoned. He kept looking for signs of recent occupancy.

This was one rotten way to territory recently held by the enemy, Rogers thought. They should have the robot "air balls" which had been so effective during the War of Liberation. Why hadn't General Gordon given them technical backup? When he got back to Niagra Rogers resolved to give Gordon the benefit of perhaps more years of experience than that general really needed. He had no way of knowing what had happened to Gordon.

"Sir," Block said over the phones, "That's good. Give us a hole into the wall on your left."

"Aknol." Rogers blasted, teleporting atoms of steel and rock atoms to distant parts. He bored carefully for nearly a minute.

"Hold it," the American called. "Let me tinker with the box here. Yeah, looks like we're getting to the far side of the mountain. There's metal or shielding below the far point of your present tunnel at—let's see. Eighty five meters. Want us to give you a hand?'-'

"Not yet." Rogers towed his *dis* gun into position and braced it to the roof of the tunnel with a magnetic grapple. The pale blue beam hissed into the rock. Minutes later he called, "This thing's shielded. The *dis* won't touch it. Now what?"

"Thermite. But first stick a mike on it and pull back."

Rogers plastered a limpet mike and flew back down the tunnel. "Would they still be active after all the noise I made burning?" he asked.

Block handed him an earphone.

"Either machinery or we've tapped a beehive."

"Bees don't use shielding," Block said. "I think we're onto something. First we report." But at that moment the command circuit came alive.

"All Apolillado units! We are engaging enemy ships your vicinity. Be alert for increased ground activity by the Han. Stay deep to avoid random *dis*.

"Marshal, we'd better cool it until this blows over."

"This may be a chance to catch them off guard. Let me have the grenades."

Six ships had appeared out of the south, stalking the coastline. Two were conventional Han walking on rep beams. Four were of a new design: faster, more streamlined, with wide tail fins and stubby wings. They were dull black and carried no insignia.

Lewis's air group attacked a hundred kilometers south of his position, streaming in from the stratsophere with combined rocket and *dis* attacks. Vidscreens in the cavern HQ were filled with sea, sky, mountains and the dark fishlike ships in formation. Rockets blossomed among them, dark smoke and débris scattered. There was a momentary closeup of the Han ships, *dis* projectors swiveling to track American fighters.

"A hit!" cried one of the rocket pilots. "Turkey aflame." One rep ray ship was smoking and falling behind. Two dark vessels faced the attackers. The group commander led an intercept, rockets firing. Hits jarred one Han but did not knock it from the sky.

"Kappa Six," Major Lewis rapped, "get that other Han transport. I have a supply group coming in from the north."

There was no reply. Viewplates gyrated with wild images as American ships passed over the Han but the pilots' chatter had ceased.

"Where's K-Six?" Lewis called. "Is that his screen?"

"Here, sir," an aide said. The screen showed blue ocean. As they watched whitecaps rushed to meet the rocket. There was a splash then the screen revealed only murk as the ship plunged deeper.

"Contact with anyone?" Lewis asked.

"Negative."

"Wiped out," the American commander whispered. They stared in silence as one ship after another went into the ocean, screen functioning, crew immobile. Major Lewis looked around. No one spoke.

"Get a fix on each of those ships!" he snarled. "Then get me Kappa One. Tell K-Three to stay on course but engage only at long range. Tell him what happened. He was probably on their frequency anyway. *Move it!*" He crouched over his table and began flipping switches.

The thermite exposed a thin and now-ruptured

webbing of wires that intact had rendered the
metal impervious to dis. He tripped the beam. The
net and underlying black metal vanished. Water
roared up the shaft, knocking Rogers aside as it
flooded the room above.

"What is it?" they called from behind.

"Free shower. Wait a minute while I turn it off."
He jumped out of the pool forming and fought his
way through the fountain to the dis controls. Protected by its own beam, the projector had not been
dislodged. He spread the beam to catch all the
water before it could reach the upper chamber.
"Must have tapped the main reservoir," he reported.

"Melt down the room you're in and seal it off,"
Block advised. "We'll try again from the east."

"Nothing doing. This is a sure entry into any
part of the complex still working. When the pressure goes down I'll go in through the pipes."

"You're crazy." The "sir" was an afterthought.

"I don't think so." Rogers grinned. "If you'll
come up here with the scope we may be able to
relay it through the reservoir or whatever it is I
hit."

"Aknol. Don't blow any more holes until we get
there."

Rogers went into the jet black water like a sal-
mon heading upstream. The cistern was big. Even
with an infra-red projector he could see no
boundary. Which way was the water supposed to
flow? His dis ray puncture had destroyed the
normal pressure dynamics, and unless he swam
constantly his belt sent him upward like a cork.
He wished he dared use jets, but even at narrowest

focus they would soon overload.

Since they all seemed equally likely he chose a pipe at random, snaked through it for a hundred meters. Then it narrowed and a dozen pipes angled off. He used his hand dis on the conduit in front of him, and it revealed only a short passage through rock before the ray hit shielding. Sure built this place to last, Rogers thought as he tossed a thermite grenade. He didn't realize he had said it aloud until Block agreed.

"HQ says those Han ships got through and are probably headed this way."

Thermite flared and Rogers probed the wreckage. He crawled out. All quiet. He scanned the chamber with infra red. "I've hit pay dirt," he whispered into the phone. "I think it's living quarters."

"They'll be coming to see who started the leak," Block warned.

Rogers edged to the door. Three more unoccupied rooms. Another door. Voices outside!

He pressed his helmet against the panel to listen. They were speaking Han—couldn't understand a word—but one voice was female. He wished he had lugged along an ultrascope. He felt the door and found the latch. It opened outward. He opened it a crack and peeked.

The room was lit. Rogers switched off his infrared and flipped up the goggles. His first glimpse showed only the flat gray surface of an instrument rack. Slowly he allowed the door to open. Three Han sat with their backs to him, on cushioned recliners before a row of vid screens which covered the entire west half of the circular room. On the center screen was a face Rogers had seen before: Mordred had survived! The Han Prince spoke in harsh tones but Rogers' interest was in one of the room's occupants. Two were men but the third . . .

Then, while Rogers watched, one Han noticed the black water that was crossing the floor. He looked around—into the muzzle of Rogers' rocket pistol.

From the man's obvious startlement, Mordred realized something was happening. He voiced a single word and the other Han dived from the couch. Without taking his eyes from the first man, Rogers shot the second. The girl turned, and as she did spoke calmly to the other Han. Both raised their hands. Behind them Mordred rapped out another question. She answered briefly, then switched to Anglish. "You die in three minutes. Is there anything you wish to say?"

Roger's voice was choked. "Ngo-Lan!"

Her eyes widened. There was a pause. Then her eyes changed. "You are mistaken," she said. "Ngo-Lan was murdered many years ago."

Rogers drew a breath. "You are my prisoners," he said. "Step away from the controls."

Prince Mordred wavered on the screen. His voice boomed and the image disappeared. The girl's face was calm but the man paled.

"Prince Mordred has armed the bomb," she said.

"What's done can be undone!" Rogers replied.

"You can return Ngo-Lan to life?"

Rogers knew he should have prepared himself. But he had spent too many years telling himself it had never happened, that he had not left her behind bound and gagged at the bottom of an elevator shaft. "Who are you?"

"My name is Lu-An. I am grandchild to Ngo-Lan."

Why hadn't he guessed it?

"I am Anthony Rogers, Lu-An. Do you know me?"

"I know only a faceless murderer who hides inside a helmet."

Rogers threw back the ultron bubble. She stepped closer and looked up into his face. He was terribly aware of the scent she wore, musklike and familiar. Her dark eyes fastened on his.

"Yes, you resemble him. But you are young. Or . . . is that your secret of eternal youth? Do you live the lives you stole from my mother, my grandmother? Have you come now to drink my blood?"

"I'm not a vampire—" he began. "It was a long time ago. I—I remember a little girl—your mother—the most charming thing in the terrible palace of the Han—except one."

"Ngo-Lan. Do you know what price she paid for your love?"

"I didn't even know she was dead. I'm glad your mother survived, Lu-An."

"She remembers the tall barbarian who was prisoner in Grandfather's palace. You frightened and fascinated her, but like Ngo-Lan, she came to love you." The girl paused, then added, "There must be a profound death wish in my bloodline."

Tony recalled himself "Lu-An, we're in another city now with an activated atomic bomb."

"I know," she said quietly. "We have only seconds."

"Lu-An, if I'd known . . . we've got to get you

out of here before that bomb goes off."

"To what end? Will you torture me? Kill me? Or have you now risen from savagery so I can live in degraded humiliation, eternally reminded of my difference?" She paused. "I think it better to die a princess than live a slave."

"Lu-An, trust me. I can prevent anything like that from happening. You'll be perfectly safe. I won't let anyone harm you."

"The eternal Rogers is reborn. Can he renew his soul? Can he stifle the narrowminded savagery of his people?"

"Yes, I can. Trust me!" The Han on the far side of the room made a sudden move. Lu-An cried out and something struck Rogers in the side. His pistol roared and the Han was dead.

"You're hurt!" the Han girl cried.

Rogers' pistol swung around and jabbed into her breast. "Did you set me up for that?"

"He had his orders."

"As you have yours?" Rogers prodded deeper with the pistol.

"Your people do not follow orders?" She gave a faint trembling smile.

Rogers was silent. It was not the first time he had been outmaneuvered by a woman . . .

Suddenly, Lu-An spoke again: "No! I do not want to die. The deactivation switch is three levels below us in the power plant. Look for a red half moon on the west wall."

"Let's move!"

A voice spoke in his ear. "HQ reports one Han ship landed on the mountainside near us. They're probably coming in to get you, Marshal, orders?"

Rogers abruptly realized that he had been hit.

But there was no pain, no limitation of movement. "Stay where you are," he muttered.

"Why am I doing this? Am I truly a coward? It cannot be simply because you are handsome that I am a traitor! No! I would rather be a coward than such a slut."

She ran, fussed with an elevator that wouldn't open, said something sincere in Han, kicked the door open, and descended a ladder, long red skirt flying around slender legs. Rogers followed, his gun in one hand. Lu-An opened another metal hatch into a curving corridor. A young Han ran around the corner. He wore black and his head was shaven. He was unarmed. Rogers waited to see if more would come.

"Sung!" the girl cried. She jumped into the path of the approaching man. The Han fell to his knees. He said something, gasped, and died. Rogers could see no wound.

Block spoke into his earphone again. "Hostiles a half kilometer down that corridor you're in. They're coming your way."

"Only one group?"

"Far's we can tell but scope penetration around you is bad. Can you shoot a few holes in the wall?"

"Later. Lu-An, what is it?"

The girl crouched by the dead man, one delicate hand on his shoulder. "The Prince has been attacked by the Prl'lu."

"The who?" Rogers thought he knew but hoped he was wrong.

"To the power room quickly!" she gasped. She ran with Rogers on her heels. She stopped at another hatch. Muttering, she spun dials. Nothing happened. She ran down the tunnel and tried another set. A light came on and far off they heard the shriek of an alarm. She ran back to the first hatch which now opened. They ducked inside. As she closed the hatch his head phones said, "Shielded area, Rogers, See you lat—"

Lu-An led him to a screen. Segments of corridor flashed as she moved controls. Suddenly there were moving figures. She focused and Rogers had his first . . . *second* glimpse of the Prl'lu. There were five Han short and slender even in black pressure suits. Behind them stalked three seven footers. The beam's resolution was poor but Rogers got an impression of large eyes with a hint of epicanthic fold, and falconlike thin Danish noses. Under transparent helmets they wore a crest of hair along an otherwise smooth skull. Their limbs were disproportionately long, and their gait totally unlike that of the Han who accompanied them.

Prince Mordred strode ahead of the others. He was taller than the other Han, as tall as Rogers. He seemed to be in command but his holster was empty.

"What're they doing down here?" Rogers asked.

"I don't know. The Prince has fallen into the hands of the strange ones. We must free him."

Rogers thought the wisdom of this move debatable. "Are they headed toward the bomb deactivator?" he asked.

"It is one level down from here. But why would they risk their lives—unless they do not know Mordred has set the bomb?"

The girl had switching screens the while to keep the party in view. Suddenly concentric circles filled the screen, there was a flash and the screen went dark.

"He is hit!" the girl cried. "This way quickly." She ran back the way they had come. Tony suspected he was making a tactical error based on a glandular response, but he sheathed his pistol and belted after her. When Lu-An threw open the hatch and jumped out Rogers flew over her head, striking a Prl'lu squarely from behind.

The lanky giant rolled into a ball, rebounded from the bulkhead and came up with a weapon in his left hand. Rogers grappled. So did the girl, both yelling.

They might as well have grabbed a high tension cable. The Prl'lu threw them across the passage. Lu-An lay unconscious. Rogers had muscle, training and body armor; he managed to stagger shakily erect. He also had Prince Mordred.

One Prl'l lay still, and as Rogers watched the other one toppled. The Prince, weapon now trained on the American, straightened from his crouch.

"Lu-An? Can you hear me?"

Stupidly, Rogers picked up the inert girl.

The prince snarled something at the several Han behind him who had not moved fast enough to please him. "Bring her," he told Rogers.

Rogers had his hands full of woman and dared not go for his gun; Mordred had already demonstrated his speed.

"Bring her," the prince repeated. His clean-shaven face was calm but his pupils dilated.

"Use that," Rogers said, "And you'll hit both of us."

"Give me the girl and I'll let you escape before the bomb explodes."

Bluffing, Rogers thought. "Lu-Ann just saved your worthless life."

"To save my life is her duty," Mordred snarled. As he raised his weapon Rogers realized he had been thinking like an eighty year old. He could take this—

"Let me put her down," Rogers said, pretending to capitulate in his own death. From his crouch Rogers dived straight at the Han prince, pistol blazing.

Mordred dodged, fired, but his bolt went wild. Han died behind him. Down the corridor a hatch flew open and two new figures appeared. Rogers' earphones were yammering. "Hang in there chief, here we come!" Block and his Peruvian teammate had arrived.

Mordred whizzed down the tunnel as if he had a powered belt. Rogers crouched to get a shot. A slim hand grabbed his wrist. He shook Lu-An loose as the soldiers reached him.

"Flee, my Prince!" Abruptly, the girl pulled herself together. "It doesn't matter," she said. "We are all doomed."

Block opened his helmet. "We disconnected the bomb. That's why we're late.

Rogers managed a ragged laugh.

IX

---◆·◆◆·◆---

"We're going after Mordred," Rogers said, "and any others of his party who remain alive. And you have demonstrated that I can't trust you."

"I have been honest with you. Did I ever promise to betray my Prince?"

"And if we run into Mordred again?"

"Will you admire me more if I deliver one of my own kind—my Prince—to gratify some glandular whim?"

Rogers suspected he was in more bondage than this girl.

"All dead, now" Block said from behind him.

Thought was so strange to Rogers that he didn't know how to put it. "Your kind? Mordred doesn't exactly look Han to me."

There was amusement in the girl's eyes as he bound and gagged her with strips of her own skirt.

"I'd have to go back to the surface to report in—" Block began. He and the Peruvian looked down at the bound Han girl with a mixture of lust and disgust.

"We can't afford to waste time," Rogers said. "Mordred's the big cheese. This is our chance to bag him." He slung Lu-An over a shoulder. "Come on."

The tunnel shuddered and rock rained through fissures in the metal walls. Rogers fell to his knees. "What the hell was that?"

Block conferred with his companion in Español. "The rest of the gang's up towards the surface, Marshal."

"Maybe Mordred had more than one bomb."

Three armored figures and one bound, unarmored girl flew single file through the tunnel system, guided through the darkness by infra-red beams. When they reached the place Block had been using as their op center the big American ultraphoned. "Hornet Six, give us a status. You guys alright?"

"Hornet, Hornet—" The signal was faint. "This is HQ, are any of you still there?"

"Hey," Block said, "That's regional command!"

Rogers put the girl down and keyed his phone. "This is Rogers. What's going on topside?"

"Glad to hear you, sir. Here's the commandant."

Major Lewis came in. "How many survivors, Marshal? We can't raise anyone else. Give us a status report on hostile ships."

"We're still underground," Rogers said. "Is the rest of my team knocked out?"

"We've had no contact."

"We'll investigate." Roger picked up Lu-An again.

"Watch your rad exposure. We A-bombed the surface.

"You what! My team was up there!"

Lewis's voice was strained. "Three missiles set for air burst. We assumed you were all dead."

The three searched but there were no survivors. He found ultron armor for Lu-An and untied her to put it on. Block ultrascoped the upper levels without result. They ascended cautiously. There was no life on the surface.

The bombing had altered the mountain. In the valley below fires smoldered in damp jungle. Rad alarms chirred in their suits. "No survivors," he told Lewis. "I need reinforcements. I have one prisoner and Mordred himself is probably trapped in the tunnels. We'll descend out of the radiation and wait for response. And you might spread the word that if this prisoner is harmed a lot of people will be harmed worse. I want prisoners and I want a stop of this endless mindless butchery!"

Lewis's voice was heavier than ever. "Aknol," he said. "But I no longer have airships. Nearest ground forces are one day from your position. Suggest you leave on foot and bring the prisoner with you."

"Aknol." Rogers switched off.

"Get what supplies you can," Rogers said to his team. "You'll go overland with Lu-An—the prisoner—while I hunt for Mordred." He was picking up Lu-An when her eyes widened. He turned as the Peruvian cried, "*Avión! Una nave del Han!*"

A tiny rep ray ship had appeared at the peak of the blasted mountain. It swing out over the valley.

Rogers dropped his disintegrator and drew his rocket pistol. The craft shot away south on angled beams as he emptied his magazine.

He paused to reload, then opened Lu-An's helmet and removed the silken gag.

"Mordred," she said. She studied Rogers with sardonic amusement. "You really don't know who he is." Then she was laughing.

The girl helped in the renewed search of Han tunnels. Within hours Rogers' team located the hangar from which Mordred had escaped. There was a clean *dis* hole in the side of the mountain. The other Han defenders were all dead.

"Your prince did this," Rogers said as they surveyed a roomful of corpses.

"Never," Lu-An said. "The Prl'lu. Mordred has escaped from them—and from you."

"Where would he go?" Rogers asked.

"I don't know." Lu-An paused, watching his face. "I would have said back to the Prl'lu base, wherever it is. But you saw—The Prl'lu had taken Mordred himself captive. When princes squabble a wise woman does not ask why." Lu-An's hair was snarled, her face and hands smudged, her dress half torn off to provide the bonds she no longer wore.

"Tell me about the Prl'lu," he began. POW interrogation seemed a particularly unsuitable vehicle for courtship but Rogers had never been a skillful suitor.

The Prl'lu, Lu-An told him, were a Han legend: a fabulous super-race who slept in a lost city that had been enchanted by remote ancestors of the Han. "The truth of these tales is known only to the ruling class, the Man-Din," she concluded, "and would not be common knowledge among the Han. Certainly not to a mere woman." She smiled. "But Mordred knew something."

Rogers was struck by the similarity to an old tale of Frederick Barbarossa and his hundred knights who slept in a magic mountain awaiting Germany's hour of peril. The only difference was that Germany had lost the Great War and no magic knights had appeared. He had seen and touched Prl'lu.

"The antarctic ice is melting," he said. "Whatever hides there will soon surface. I suspect it poses as much threat to the Han as to the rest of us."

"I fear Mordred has so discovered," the girl said. "But he would open hell to get at you, Rogers."

Rogers sighed. He was inured to the adulation bestowed on him by hero-worshiping humans, but such hatred puzzled him. "Now that Mordred has escaped will you give me your parole and accompany us without trying to escape?"

"Can I trust you to protect me? I am pure Han."

"Dear Lu-An," He took her hand. "I will allow nothing to harm you whether you cooperate or not. Do not fear. I am in command of the American forces and you are under my personal protection." As he promised Rogers hoped he could deliver.

Entallador's jungle scouts found them before they had belted seventy kilometers. Rogers' *salvoconducto* for his prisoner would have been challenged had not Major Lewis and Boss Entallador both issued the strictest orders.

From the Peruvians Rogers' party got more news of the débacle of Lewis's air force, but Rogers only got full details when he reached the cave headquarters. "So what's new about death rays?" he asked. "*Dis* does it all."

"These rays kill the pilots but don't damage ships or real estate." Lewis paused. "Shows you what's improtant."

Rogers wondered how the uninventive Han had come up with a new weapon.

"What you call the Prl'lu," Lewis said. "All my ships were wiped out in their initial assault. The Han landed at your mountain. We vaporized one or two of them, but they killed all our troops on the surface. Afterward there were reports of ships heading north, heading south—I don't know where they are. Niagra's sending me a new squadron, but very reluctantly." He gestured toward his map. "I'm holding a picket line and have orders to A-bomb anything that moves. God help the poor natives. You've seen these Prl'lu. What can you tell me?"

"Not much. We're fighting a bogeyman the Han use to scare their kids. Lu-An didn't think they were real until . . . They're nothing like the Han. They're fast, tough, and deadly. That character who lassoed my ship down in the antarctic ice must have been a Prl'lu." He told the story and Lewis was impressed.

"Marshal," he said, "the best place for you is back at Niagra building a fire under the council. Much as I could use you here, you'd better jet."

Reluctantly, Rogers agreed. "I'll take my scout ship and my prisoner."

Three senior officers and six armed troopers met him at Niagra. His briefing was quick. General Gordon's death was a blow. Gordon had been a friend and ally. Also, Rogers realized, that purulent mass of rioting carcinoma could just as easily have been himself.

He saw to Lu-An's placement in a guarded suite at the Citadel, then scheduled his meeting with the council. Then he shut himself in his office and made two calls.

"Ruth," he said, cutting short her expressions of happiness that he still lived. "I need your advice. Can you fly over to see me?"

"When?"

"Now. I have to address the council tomorrow."

"I'll be there."

"Lieutenant Holcomb reporting . . . Tony, is that you? Thank God! Rumor has the entire Peruvian base wiped out."

"I've got a letter from her for you." Rogers smiled in spite of himself. "Whatever your assignment is now, forget it. You're back on my staff. I want you with me when I go before the council tomorrow. How's your arm?"

"Healing. See?" He saluted.

"Get it back in a sling."

"Huh?"

"It's not enough to be a wounded hero. Tomorrow I want you to look like one."

"Aye, aye, sir."

"Get over here on the double. Beam off."

Rogers had time to confer with Holcomb before

Ruth arrived. His conference with Dr. Harris lasted all night.

"Tony, this Pru'lu legend makes it sound like the Han have been here for a long time."

"I thought they arrived by meteorite or something into Central China just a few centuries ago."

"That's the tradition. But why would they believe in a hidden super race?"

"Not exactly my line," Rogers said. "But don't most people tell stories like that?"

When she stared he told her the ancient story of the redbearded kaiser and his hundred knights.

"Earth must have been a wonderful place when there were so many people and so much history."

Rogers remembered the Great War and thought it was not too different from the present. "Maybe they brought the story with them from wherever the Han came from?"

"But there *is* a super race."

"And Mordred knew."

"Yes, Tony, and what else has been hidden all these centuries?"

"What?"

"That suspended animation chamber you popped into in 1927."

"The Han had something to do with that?"

"Or the Prl'lu. What did they look like?"

Rogers described them.

"And nobody with enough curiosity to bring back a body for study!" Ruth mourned. "It's no wonder we lose the war. We should be taking prisoners, interrogating, learning everything we can of the enemy."

"I took a prisoner."

"A Han? What does he think they are?"

"She. They come in both sexes, just as we do. In combat you take what you can get." Rogers decided there was no reason for Ruth to know how he felt about Lu-An. With a transparent effort to change the subject he asked how General Gordon had died. The details sickened him. It could have been Rogers.

"Going to miss him," he said inadequately. "And tomorrow before the council I could have used his help." He paused. "We have to get Dr. Wolsky in on this."

"Convince him that the Prl'lu made his precious chamber and you won't be able to keep him out."

"I mean the death ray too. Would he be the right person to study that?"

"It's right down his line. Do they have the bodies of any of those poor airmen?"

Rogers didn't know. "Maybe they've been able to salvage some of Lewis's ships. I'll find out."

Marshal Anthony Rogers took the seat at the head of the horseshoe shaped table. Dapper in uniform and khaki arm sling, Holcomb stood behind him. Status reports flashed over vidscreens at the far end of the chamber. Most of the council and staff were ready. General Gordon's seat held a young colonel Rogers had not met before.

There had been a hush as Rogers entered. Many had not seen him since his transformation. Another card, Rogers mused—if only he knew how to play it. He nodded briefly to Major Dupre. The carefully groomed woman activated a screen and Lewis's face appeared.

"Progress report October tenth, twenty four

seventy six," he began. A map appeared. Lewis gave a grim recital of reversals and disasters. He concluded with a request for reinforcements.

"I'd like to hear from the air force boss," Rogers said.

"We have urgent reports on sea level changes first," Major Dupre said.

Rogers nodded. A new map filled the screen. There were evacuation reports. A geologist estimated the effects of melting the south polar ice cap and showed a new world map with much less land. "And if the Greenland ice cap is added to that?" Rogers asked.

"The east coast of the United States will disappear, save for mountainous areas. The Gulf of Mexico and Hudson's Bay will join. The west coast will recede to the Rockies. The rest of the world—"

"Never mind," Rogers said smoothly. His purpose was accomplished.

Reports followed: troop and rocket ship assignments, intelligence estimates of the Prl'lu, which Niagra preferred to call "the Antarctic Han."

"Any autopsy data on the crews of Major Lewis's lost squadron?" Rogers remembered Ruth's suggestion.

"Neg, Marshal. Ships have not been retrieved."

As the reports continued Roger wrote a note and handed it over his shoulder to Holcomb.

Have Wolsky on the line, it said. *Call Entallador. Get names two SA bosses we can call for polit. est. Now.* Holcomb quietly ushered himself out of the room.

Positions shaped up rapidly. Airships and resources were, as always, in short supply: guarding the air approaches to the "North American Bastion" was top priority. All forces would be withdrawn from South America and the rest of the world and placed in a defensive screen at America's borders.

Money and personnel were to be withdrawn from all research, including the *Wilma Deering* and diverted to rocket ship and weapons production. Once North America and especially Niagra was safe they could think about aggressive responses to the new Han menace.

They had forgotten the South Americans and they had forgotten that Niagra would soon be under water. Where the hell, Rogers wondered, was Holcomb? Where were Drs. Harris and Wolsky? Someday these shortsighted isolationists might come rowing their boat to the high peaks of the Andes. It would serve them right if the only land left was occupied by either the Han or embittered Latinos.

"Ladies and gentlemen," Rogers began, "Do you remember what it took to defeat the first Han empire? Inertron and ultron shielding protected us from the dis ray. Our rocket artillery could surround the Han with a wall of fire. We had the ultraphone, which gave us interception-proof, jam-proof communications. And we had brave Americans able to see beyond their noses. What has happened?

"Only a generation later we face a recrudescence of the Han menace. We still have heroes. Lieutenant Holcomb stands behind me, living proof. But the Han have violated our communications security. Since they broadcast on it, we must assume they monitor the ultraphone as well. Their allies kill us inside armored ships. They have rays, bombs, gas, ships—all better than ours. And they are melting the polar ice to drown half the world!" He paused to glance at the note Holcomb slipped him.

"Now is no time to let up on research," he continued. "We must learn to neutralize the advantages our enemies have obtained. We must understand polar phenomena. We must understand the underground fortresses of the Han. We need the enemy's death ray. We need polar exploration and to look into the subsurface installation Dr. Harris tells me has been found less than two hundred miles from where I sit."

The council stirred but Rogers rushed on. "By all estimates, the enemy is few in numbers. Now is no time to retreat into a defensive posture and let Prince Mordred take over the world. We have brave young men and women; we have allies. We have heroes. We have scientific genius. Let us move forward to defeat the Han."

Rogers gave them only seconds to react, then turned to the vidscreen and brought on several South American bosses to respond to the proposed withdrawal. Entallador made a reasoned but emotional appeal for support of his embattled people. An old Amazonian politico told the council what he thought of the withdrawal of North American air power when he had been forbidden to develop his own air force. He also pointed out that he was closer to the Andes and once he had evacuated his low-lying country the norteameri-

canos could tread water: they would not get into the South American highlands.

Rogers got Holcomb's attention. "Do you know Major Dupre's aide?"

"Only slightly," the lieutenant whispered.

"Tell her Wolsky's learning how to control the rejuvenation chamber."

"Is he, sir?"

"Who cares—we need that old barracuda's vote."

The conference lasted most of the afternoon. When it was over Rogers was exhausted but triumphant. "We got an increase in the Peruvian garrison, an expedition to the pole, a search party for Lewis's downed ships, and a commitment to more research," he told Ruth later.

"Thanks to your skill."

"Thanks to kissing generals. And now I've got to go nail them all down. With luck I'll be free in a few hours. Dinner?"

"I'll be here," she promised.

Two of Rogers' post-conference calls were special. One was to the communications base at the Citadel. "You've got a tech here named Jerina?"

"Right, Marshal," the woman replied. "Do you want to see him? He's on duty."

"Please."

When the young trooper entered Rogers gave a quick salute and grasped his hand. "Your quick thinking saved Lieutenant Holcomb's life and probably mine." He told the story to the technician's superior and departed with a final thanks.

"Loyalty must be rewarded," he remarked to Holcomb as they shot down a drop tube. "Always remember."

"Aye, sir."

"And now," Rogers said as an armed guard approached them down the corridor, "I'll handle this mission alone. See you in my office in six hours."

"Yes sir." Holcomb jumped back up to the upper levels.

"Lu-An," Rogers said when they were alone in her prison suite, "The Prl'lu: surely you can help me find and destroy their base without disloyalty to the Han cause."

Locked away from any contact but female guards, the prisoner had amused herself creating a new wardrobe from the utilitarian clothing provided her. She wore a skintight bodice of black which complemented long jet hair. From hips down she was encased in a translucent silk-like garment which did not detract from long straight legs. Like an illustration from *The Arabian Nights*, Rogers thought.

She was sullen and uncommunicative.

"What's wrong?"

"Where have you been for two days?" the girl cried. "Why have you left me alone and helpless? What have you been doing?" She gazed into his face. "You have another woman!"

Rogers gave a guilty start. He had never understood that with a functional uterus it does not require evidence to draw this conclusion. "Lu-An," he protested, "you never gave me any reason to believe you had such emotions toward me."

"Ah!" She stalked about throwing pillows, portable communicator, and a vase. "Field Marshal Anthony Rogers, the most powerful man in the Northern Hemisphere! Greatest military strategist of the human race! The Han will devour you. I should have stayed in the mountain."

He seized her arm. "You would not have died in any case. We inactivated the bomb." But logic versus passion had been equally unavailing with Wilma. If this young lady was surrendering to her glands Rogers might as well meet her terms. He put his arms around her and the mood changed. Then he saw her looking up. "What is it?"

"There is a snoop focused on this room."

"It's turned off as long as I'm here."

"Will they obey you?"

"They better."

Lu-An had more common sense than the Supreme Commander. She pushed him away and spent the next ten minutes stuffing rags into the opening of every snoop lens. Then her arms stole round his neck and drew him close.

In his excitement he called her Ngo-Lan. She laughed. "Am I so like my grandmother?"

X

---•◆•◆•◆•---

"The archives were destroyed in the war," Lu-An said. "They were in China, in the City of the Birthplace."

"I remember that city," Rogers said. "It was flattened."

Lu-An sighed. "All the beautiful cities: Ho-Khan, Lo-Tan, Nu-Yok; their towers and spires, parks, walkways, all smashed by the bloodthirsty rage of your Americans."

"All rotten," he protested, "Based on suppression of the Ku-li by the ruling class, riddled with intrigue and founded on the total suppression of the human race. What did you expect of us—that we would offer to kiss and make up?"

"All right, Rogers," the girl sighed. "Make me no speeches. Ho-Khan was destroyed. Its library and computers are gone. We believe all the information was duplicated in other computers. Somewhere Mordred found a key to the myth of the Prl'lu. I doubt it was in Khai-Ton. That was a new city—one old San-Lan built in the last few months of the war."

"I thought we had destroyed all of them," Rogers mused. "How many were there? Is that South American stronghold the only surviving Han base?"

"The only one."

He could not tell if she was lying.

"Ngo-Lan and others from the palace fled there during the fearsome attack of the floating missiles," she went on. "The tunnels were blowing up behind them; thousands were being crushed. My mother told me that the screams went on for hours." She shuddered. "There were ultrafast rail cars for the Imperial Household; a few escaped to South America. Mordred was born there." She looked into Rogers' eyes. "That is all I know."

It was not all she knew. Rogers remembered her amusement each time he mentioned Mordred.

Holcomb was aching for action. "The *Eagle* is repaired, sir. We're ready."

Rogers handed him a set of photographs. "These were taken by stratosphere scout," he said. "The ice cap is mostly gone, and we know where the energy is coming from. Look, here's an infra-red shot of the South Pole. See those ten hot spots where the surface is bare rock?"

"Where did we run into the Prl'lu when my ship went down?" Holcomb asked.

"Here's where your beacon dropped. Nothing but bare rock there too."

"When these Prl'lu decide to clean up they do a thorough job," Holcomb said. "Tony, we know they're under there. Let's *dis* a few holes in the rock."

"We can't send ships in when the Prl'lu can kill at a distance and we have no defense."

"They may only have one of those death rays," Holcomb argued. "Maybe it got blown up in the Mount Apolillado strike."

Rogers pointed to his map. "I've got a thousand Americans with flying belts and rocket artillery moving into Entallador's area. We're going to dig out every Han in South America. Then we will take on Antarctica. By then I hope we'll have enough flying eye airballs to make most of the assault by remote control. Meanwhile Wolsky may give us something on the death ray." He rummaged through reports on his desk. "We did have a report from him, didn't we?"

"Yes, sir. He's at the mine in Pennsylvania."

"Let's try out your ship. Get Captain Targ and arrange for messages to be relayed to the Eagle. I have to make calls to Dr. Harris and the security block. Get cracking."

"Yes sir," the airman grinned.

They could already see steam rising above the green forested mountains even before the Eagle had climbed high enough to give a clear view: the sea had come up the narrow valley to the very entrance of the mine. Here dis projectors had been placed and the rising tide now poured into a gigantic trench dug across the valley. Intermittent dis snapped on to disperse the water that poured steadily over the far edge of the trench.

Holcomb brought the Eagle low over the mine head and hovered. Rogers opened the ultron canopy and jumped a hundred meters to the ground. He was met by a young soldier who saluted snappily. "Dr. Wolsky?" Rogers had to shout over the cascading waters and intermittent thunderclaps of dis.

"In the mine," she yelled. "This way, sir."

The mine shaft was confusion. Water seeping through walls created a stream of mud. Wet and disgruntled soldiers and students horsed equipment to the shaft, then floated it up on ropes with inertron lifters. Dr. Wolsky was at the bottom where a small dis ray controlled the rapidly accumulating flood. The rejuvenation chamber had been partially dismantled, but several bulky unknown machines still stood in the excavation, now in several centimeters of water.

"How long has this been going on?" Rogers asked.

The little scientist was happy to see him. "The tide arrived two days ago. We control it with the disintegrators sent by your friend, Major Dupre, but now—" He gestured. "Walls start to fall in so already I evacuate."

"Tough luck, Doc. Can I help?"

The scientist looked desperate. "You can see these things," He gestured to the enigmatic devices in the pit. "are never to go up the small hole through which we descend. But the military minds up topside—they do not want to burn their way in here!"

"What'll happen if dis hits one of those machines, Doc?" Rogers sloshed forward to peer into the chamber.

"Nothing. We tried to get you out with a dis ray beam."

"Be quicker to clear people away from topside

and shoot *dis* from down here than to convince any military committee," Rogers said.

"I had not thought of that," Wolsky said.

It took a sizeable team to get the immensely heavy machines out of a *dis* crater. When Rogers and Holcomb finally left, Wolsky and the officer in charge of Operation Canute were organizing an overland two to get the equipment across the mountains.

Rogers belted back up to the *Eagle* and pulled off his boots. "You restocked the ship, Will. I have just one question."

"Sir?"

"Any dry socks?"

Dr. Harris had covered one wall of her office with a blackboard, then covered that with equations. Paper littered the floor and her desk top. She smiled vaguely when Rogers and Holcomb entered.

"What is all this?" he asked.

"The interdimensional problem," she sighed. "At least once a year I have an attack of it. Something about the stuff Wolsky's been bringing in got me started again."

"Is this practical? Does it have anything to do with the war effort?"

"Where inertron comes from? How does the ultra-beam radio work? What is the nature of reality? It has to do with everything. I think it especially has to do with the nature of that time stasis field in Pennsylvania you fell out of to ruin my reputation."

"So it was a dumb question," Rogers said. "What does Wolsky say? We just pulled him out of a hole in the seashore."

"You did what?"

"The seashore is against the Appalachians now. We had to dig him out before he went under."

"My goodness, Tony, is he alright?"

"Sure. But who can say what it did to those machines? What did he say that set you off on this snark hunt?"

"I'll be available on ultra beam if you need the ship," Holcomb interrupted.

"Aknol."

Later, Harris and Rogers sat in a darkened laboratory as Wolsky and a pathologist named Tanaka went through endless slides on the vidscreen. The body of one of the pilots from the death ray squadron had been retrieved from his downed ship and submitted to an analysis of which Wolsky had said, "You wouldn't like the details, so don't ask."

"—suggestive of anoxia," the pathologist finished.

Wolsky's objected: "Anybody dead you could say that. This was a healthy man. You think respiratory or cardiac?"

"Well, I can speculate—"

"We are not asking you to publish, Doctor. Give us your opinion."

"Neural shock followed by cardiac arrest."

Wolsky questioned immediately with: "Like electric shock, you mean?"

"No. I've the lysosome pattern for that and it was not electricity. But it had to be sudden, as you suggest." The pathologist fiddled with controls and selected a picture of brown and green blobs on a purple background. "Look here at the depletion of these pinealocytes."

"What does that mean? I don't follow your area too close," Wolsky queried.

"Nor-epi." The pathologist hesitated. "Of course I'm not sure."

"Of course you're not," Ruth interjected. "You've only seen one case. Would nor-epinephrine do it? I mean, is there enough even if it were all released?"

The slide changed. "There's the content," Tanaka said, "not much of a rise. But he's been days in the water."

"We know," Wolsky said. "Can you try it by experiment?"

"I suppose so—by injection. But I don't know how the pineal or any of the brainstem nuclei could be persuaded to release all their transmitter at once."

"I wish I knew the magnetic resonance and spin of the molecule," Dr. Harris said musingly.

"Tomorrow," Wolsky volunteered. "The computer is down for the night. All right, enough! Thank you a million times, Dr. Tanaka. Tomorrow we inject rabbits. Ruth, you think of a way to get massive release in milliseconds?"

"I think so. Come on, Tony, the party's over."

"Do they have an answer?" he asked. "More important, can you create a countermeasure?" Rogers asked as they walked across the grass. Acting as bodyguard, Holcomb followed.

"This is all just speculation," she began.

"Put it as simply as you can."

"Tanaka thinks something destroyed the pineal gland; that released nor-epi into the brain. This could cause cardiac arrest."

"The gland can't be very big. How did they hit such a tiny target through the wall of a moving ship?"

"Certain organic molecules are the upper limit of dis beam teleportation. It's as though the beam homed in on them."

"By which you mean anything more complex is broken down by the beam?"

She nodded.

"You're assuming an ultrabeamed and highly selective dis effect. Is that possible?"

"Theoretically."

"Can we shield against it? I don't want things ultrabeamed into me."

"I don't think there's any way to shield." She broke off. "I'd better not say that."

"Progress?"

"We're speculating, Tony. I must tell you something about scientific speculation."

"What's that?"

"It's almost always wrong."

The vidscreen in Ruth Harris's apartment was flashing as they entered. Dr. Wolsky's worried face appeared. "Calling you and the military base at Niagra Central," the image said. "My crew was hit by rep ray ships at twenty-one-oh-eight when crossing the mountains with salvaged gear. Position seventy-seven-thirty five, forty-two-twenty-two. End recording. Beam me."

Rogers tapped in his personal code and got

comcentral at Niagra. "Get a fix on that?" he asked. "What action has been taken?"

"No report after first message, sir. Captain Nogales is aloft over Florida. He's rocketing to their last reported position. HQ is skying two swoopers. The RB-25 is at base, but still on the tarmac."

"Get me the duty officer."

"Aye, sir."

Rogers triggered his chest mike and got Holcomb. "Back to Ruth's place on the jump." The screen now showed the com room boss.

"Priority red," Rogers said. "Tell RB-25 to lift and proceed on an inland search pattern. And get the tactics boss to plot an intercept across the Caribbean and Central Am. The *Eagle* will take the shoreline. Build a fire under those swooper scouts. We need intelligence."

"Aknol, sir."

There was a knock at the door. Ruth admitted a flushed Holcomb. "Back to Entallador's?"

Rogers allowed himself a brief laugh. "Pennsylvania. And I'll bet this was Mordred's work, not the Prl'lu." He kissed Ruth and they jetted into the night sky.

The RB-25 was an experimental rocket-battleship equipped with Harris effect motors and Han rep ray beams. It looked like a finned dumbbell as it rose, searchlights ablaze and rocketed south. The ship was armed with *dis* ray batteries, rocket launchers with conventional big-bang missiles and a new acid-containing missile designed to attack ray shielding.

Aboard the *Eagle*, Holcomb got a fix on the

RB-25, the three ships coming up from the south, and the two scouts fanning out from Niagra with the *Eagle*. Green and blue dots swarmed across the plate. The rest was darkness. Repeatedly, he scoped the skyline as Rogers piloted southeast toward the encroaching Atlantic.

Niagra had been moved several times during the centuries and now lay north and west of its position during Rogers' first avatar. Beneath, the dark forests of North America showed no lights.

Rogers glanced at the plot. "Where do you think he's heading?"

"He'll be loaded down if he got all of Wolsky's stuff."

"We'll have to assume he did. We had no report since Wolsky's people were first hit."

"Damn! I'll bet he has another secret base in Central America."

"Possible," Rogers admitted.

"Then he'd run for the sea and sneak south."

Hours dragged. A scout reached the scene of the Han attack. The equipment was gone. *"Dis,"* the pilot beamed, "No sign of survivors. I'll land and search."

"Another ship lost to our search grid," Holcomb grumbled.

"Can't be helped. What's that?"

"That" was a red dot at the extreme range of the ultra-probe. While Holcomb manned the controls Rogers watched the trace wink in and out. The range was right. A conventional rep ray ship can only make two hundred kilometers an hour and they had taken time to load.

"Maybe they dissed the stuff," Holcomb suggested.

"It's indestructible," Rogers said. Wolsky tried. "Besides, if they made the raid they must want it." He paused. "It's got to be a manned ship. No jury rigged robot could steal ten sledloads of junk."

"Trying to evade," Holcomb said a moment later.

"The trace is stronger. Locked onto him!" Rogers keyed the ultraphone. "Blue Six, we have a single target." He rattled off coordinates and velocity. "Red four, detach one ship to intercept; the rest of you maintain search pattern. This may be a ruse."

Their quarry turned west and as dawn brightened the clouds over the eastern rim the *Eagle* swept over the new shoreline of the southeastern coast of America in pursuit of the enemy.

"I can't recognize the coastline," Rogers broadcast, "But we're somewhere over the KenTenn gang's area. Niagra, get me the local boss."

Most twenty fifth century Americans were cleanshaven but the man whose face appeared on the screen had a curly black beard around his black face. "Good morning, Marshal," he said. "What can I do for you at this hour?"

"You have a Han ship over your territory." Rogers gave details. By the time the *Eagle* came within visual range the rep ray ship was taking rocket fire from the ground.

"We're almost in range," Holcomb broke in.

"Hold off, Will. Red Four should be in sight shortly; we'll hit him together."

Dis lashed out at them as the two American ships converged on the enemy ship, but the range was too great, and the Han was soon beyond range of the ground gunners as well, and the battle turned purely aerial.

During a pause in the action the other rocket ship swooped and came level with the *Eagle*. Roger's ultraphone showed the face of a young woman, long yellow hair billowing from her helmet.

"Red Alpha Four reporting."

"Thank you, Alpha. You will make the first run with the rockets. We'll follow up with *dis*. Proceed." The other ship peeled off and the *Eagle* followed. The Han was still climbing.

"We have you on scope," a new voice called as the first rockets burst over the enemy ship. "This is RB-25. Visual contact in three minutes."

"Aknol," Rogers called. Ahead of them the little American rocket ship wheeled from the Han.

"No hits," Rogers commented. He fired missiles from his own wing launchers and the *Eagle* pulled out of her run.

"He just hit Red Alpha," Holcomb said.

"I've lost altitude," the other American reported. "Hold onto him. I'll follow."

Southeast the Han invader stalked, *rep* rays almost invisible in the morning sun. *Dis* crashed and shells thundered but both Han and American armor held. Then the dumbbell shape of RB-25 came through low level cumulus over Tennessee.

"Clear sky for the first salvo!" the dreadnaught's gunnery officer called. "Scouts away!"

"Good shooting," Rogers called. "We can't touch him."

The Han swung his *dis* against this new opponent as explosives and acid rained against his

armor plate. *Dis* cracked and roared. The smaller
ships stood off and hovered. Smoke burst from the
Han.

"Holed him!" Holcomb cried.

"Keeping his altitude though," Rogers noted.
"Somebody on that ship knows how to fly." The
enemy still stood on its rep rays when the American commander whipped out with a blast of his
own repellor rays. Pale purple caught the Han
broadside and he reeled. The American was
thrown back but blasted with rockets and held
position.

"Push him down," Holcomb said. "Look at
that!"

"As long as he's got more power," Rogers
agreed.

The Han ship went into a roll and the American
slammed more rep into it; the Han hit the ground
hard but still balanced on two rep beams. *Dis* rays
crackled. Hillside forest dissolved.

"He's burrowing in!" Rogers cried. "Don't let
him get away, RB-25. He's trying to tunnel!"

"I'm working on it, sir." The ground below was
riddled with acid shells.

"Got him!" the battleship captain exulted.
"Now we'll drop to one thousand and *dis* him
close-focus."

The Han ship fell smoking into a selfcreated
chasm. "No—stand off. We're going in after prisoners," Rogers called.

"Right, Marshal, Cease fire all batteries. Rep, hit
him again if he tries to come out."

Holcomb grounded the *Eagle* at the edge of the
devastation and Rogers was opening the canopy
when a new voice came on the phone. "Field

Marshal Anthony Rogers of North America?"

There was only one voice like that. The screen remained blank. Rogers paused, hand still on the latch.

"Rogers?" the voice was weaker.

"I'm here."

"Are you outside?"

"Yes."

"This is Imperial Prince Mordred. I am hit. I will surrender the ship to you personally, and to you only. Come aboard alone." The hiss of dis from the buried ship stopped.

"Tony, it's a trap," Holcomb said.

Rogers knew it was a trap, but he also knew that capturing Mordred alive might mean the salvation of humanity. He was acting against his better judgment, but: "All right, Mordred," Rogers called. "I'm coming in."

XI

The ground was torn and broken; great brown gashes in green Tennessee hills led to the hole into which the Han ship had retreated. Rogers adjusted his light and belt, drew his rocket pistol and floated down.

The ship had done a good job of burying itself; he went eighty meters into the earth before he saw the first glint of metal. As he approached, a hatch opened and yellow light streamed out.

"Come in, Rogers." The disembodied voice was Mordred's. "The control room is to your right."

Rogers flicked off his chest light and stepped cautiously inside. Nothing moved: the brightly lit compartment was empty, the door at its other end shut. He opened the door: more equipment; conduits; instruments—but no Han. Room by room he advanced toward the nose. Wolsky's machines were stored amidships, banded to the steel deck. They looked undamaged.

The control room, like those of most Han airships, was without windows; the bulkheads lined with vidplates. Before each was a recliner. Only

one chair was occupied. Mordred slouched,
empty hands displayed. The chair was swiveled
to face the approaching Rogers.

"Enter," said the prince of the Han. "So it *was*
you in the tunnels of Apolillado. Had I recognized
you, you would not have escaped alive."

"We were both fortunate to escape. Where are
your men, Mordred? You didn't fly this mission
alone."

"I have dismissed them." The slender black
clad figure did not move except to speak.

"Marshal," a new voice came over Rogers' ultraphone. "Twitchell in the RB-25. There's tun-
neling going on southeast from the ship. Gone a
hundred meters already."

"Keep on top of them," Rogers said. "If they try
to surface, let them have it." His eyes flashed to
Mordred. "Whatever your proposal is, let's have it
quickly." He studied his enemy. The man seemed
young, but fine wrinkles around his eyes
suggested that he was not. Shoulder length jet
hair was pulled back from his fine featured face
into a chignon. Eyes of a startling icy gray gazed
unblinking into Rogers'.

"My proposal," Mordred said, "is that we join
forces to stop the Prl'lu who now menace the
entire planet. I will give you the secret of their
death ray if you will attack and destroy the magma
pumping station beneath Antarctica."

If enemies had enough in common to become
allies under a common threat, Rogers wondered
why they had fought in the first place. But to
dwell overlong on this could give him migraine.
"I will accept," he said, "providing you remain
hostage in Niagra."

Mordred's smile was not amused. "The Emperor of the Han should give his person into your hands? You fool, you are in my power! I can destroy this ship in fifty milliseconds. Agree to my terms or be incinerated along with the Prl'lu apparatus that has given you your contradictory existence on this plane of temporality."

"If I were as all powerful as the Han emperor I might agree," Rogers said equably. "But some semblance of democracy still lives in America. If you do not return to Niagra, any pact I make will be overruled." Dear me, he was turning pompous again.

"Marshal Rogers," the commander's voice came again, "I don't know what they're using in that tunnel but they've gone another half kilometer. They'll be over the horizon before we know it."

"Have Holcomb and the Red Squadron—" Rogers began, when:

"Rogers, your decision! The details of this agreement can wait til later, if we both survive."

"Give me the formula for the death ray and the coordinates of the ice melting station," Rogers said. "I'll agree to a nonagression policy toward any Han cities now extant, including the one in Peru currently under my control." And pray the council goes along.

Mordred smiled. "And in addition you will release the Princess Lu-An of the royal imperial line and deliver her immediately into my keeping." He said carefully, "I don't want to see her hurt."

"The girl is guilty of treason. She will be tried with all the circumstance befitting her rank."

"Red six reports unidentified aircraft approaching supersonic out of the northeast," the ul-traphone interrupted. "I will move to intercept."

"The Prl'lu have spotted us!" Mordred cried. "The game is up. The antarctic base is at Mount Erebus."

"Negative, RB-25!" Rogers ignored Mordred. "Don't engage, you haven't a chance. All units, Red, Alpha, Holcomb, jet out of here. I'll evacuate with the Prince. Jet out! That's an order!"

"You're trapped, Rogers," Mordred's joy was unholy.

The lights went out. Rogers fired into the dark as the hatch behind him slammed. In the closed compartment the explosion deafened him. Then when he knew he would hear again the first he heard was Mordred's silky voice saying *"I am your son!"*

He turned on his light. The chair was de-molished along with the instruments behind it. The cabin was filled with smoke. There was no Mordred alive or dead. A highpitched whine be-gan. Instrument lights flared red.

Ears still ringing, Rogers turned toward the re-ported escape channel. With his left hand he drew a portable *dis*. With his right he fired rockets into the bulkhead, then followed up with *dis*. Metal began to erode. The black tunnel loomed before him. He belted off after the escaping Han. Behind him the red glow of the melting ship soon faded. "Fifty milliseconds was a gross underestimate," Rogers growled.

But Mordred had made a clean escape. In half an hour Rogers despaired of ever catching up. He turned back down the tunnel. He was too late: The

Prl'lu had put six *dis* holes through the melted wreckage. Rogers flew up and caught the chatter of fighter pilots above. He spotted four American rockets hovering.

"I told them you were indestructible," Holcomb said. He brought the *Eagle* down to jump distance. "But when we slipped back and found the black ship gone and the wreck still molten and no sign of Rogers I must admit I had a moment of doubt."

"I didn't catch Mordred," Rogers said dispiritedly. "He didn't catch me, and the Prl'lu didn't catch either of us. The Prl'lu, I suspect, got the apparatus they were looking for. And I got a little information out of Mordred."

"We got a complete pickup on your conversation," Holcomb said. "Do you think he meant it?"

Rogers had been hoping nobody would know what had passed between him and the Han prince, but with mikes keyed it was impossible to keep secrets. Now rumors would spread and grow and the louder he denied, the faster they would fly. He had had time to think over Mordred's last remark. Lu-An had told him Ngo-Lan had survived the destruction of the Han stronghold. She could have been with child at the time. His? Well, yes, it was possible; the extent of his liaison with the Emperor's favorite had never been revealed. Especially not to Wilma, whose arrival had interrupted their attempt to escape together, and forced Rogers to leave his quondam lover in the lurch.

His account of that incident in his official memoirs had been pure fantasy. He could not tell

his adopted people—much less his wife—that he
had been intimate with their hereditary enemies.
So he had lied.

The Han were inhumanly longlived. If he had a
child by Ngo-Lan, that child could easily be
Mordred. What the hell kind of a name was that? It
wasn't Han.

"Mordred is mad," he told Holcomb. "Fur-
thermore, he'd say anything to gain the advantage
of surprise. Anything. That's my official opinion
and my last word on the subject."

"Yes sir. Do you think he got away?"

Rogers looked sourly at his inquisitor. "He
left first. If I got away before the Prl'lu arrived I
must suppose he did. Did you trace the escape
tunnel?"

"Twitchell lost it under the Atlantic. They must
have a *dis* equipped airship aboard."

"It strikes me now that all the time we talked,
Mordred never moved . . . I wonder if I was talking to him or some kind of a projected illusion."

"Are such things possible?" Holcomb asked.

"In 1927 we knew movies would never talk."
Rogers had to explain then what movies used to
be. "Ask Dr. Harris if it's possible," he said. *And
I'll ask Lu-An.*

"It was not necessary for her to tell everyone he
was your son," Lu-An said. "Look in the mirror.
Besides, would a stranger dedicate his life to destroying you? Do you not know that close hates
are best?"

"Why have you never told me this?" Rogers
cried. "What earthly purpose was there in keeping it secret?"

"Should I tell a five hundred year old man what he does not wish to see?" she asked. "In any event, I did not think it important."

"You didn't think? You never stop thinking! There must be another reason!"

"I am Han. Is my whole life, every memory and loyalty to be erased because I surrender to the pleasures of the flesh?"

"Mordred knew precisely when it was that we lifted the gear out of the mine," Rogers said. "Out of consideration for your feelings, I have never subjected you to a complete body scan." He opened the door of the apartment. "Guard!"

She said tiredly, "Who tells me anything in this prison? Did I know your plans? But of course I have a microtransmitter in my skull. I've worn it since I was twelve like any Han."

"Mordred has been listening to you—to us making love!"

The guard appeared in the doorway. "Sir?" she asked.

"Take the prisoner to medical, please. Full scan for implanted devices."

"Very good, sir." She reached for Lu-An's wrist.

"Take her away!" Rogers cried.

As Rogers walked into his office three people got to their feet. He paused, heavy with depression and fatigue. Ruth Harris took his arm, kissed him, and led him to his seat.

"I'm alright," he said. Holcomb and Wolsky resumed their chairs. He tried to relax, turn off his memory.

"Ruth, what does Mordred mean? That's not a Han name."

"He was the—the natural son of Arthur, King of Britain in old British legend."

"They fought?"

"They killed each other."

"That fits," he said bitterly. "But I wonder what the name means."

"Arthur and Mordred did not speak Anglish," Wolsky said unexpectedly. "They spoke an older Celtic tongue which I once studied."

"And Mordred?"

"Literally, I think it would mean *Big Trouble*."

Nobody laughed.

Rogers sighed. "What about Mount Erebus?"

"Extinct volcano in Antarctica," Ruth said. "Centuries ago when Ross discovered it, Mount Erebus was still active."

"And that fits. Could Mordred have created some kind of three dimensional image of himself so lifelike I'd think it was real?"

"Before the Great Disaster there was some experimental 3-D imagery with lasers," she said. "The technique is lost."

"Dr. Wolsky, I'm sorry about losing your equipment. Sorrier yet about losing your people. It was misjudgment on my part."

"Nonsense, Marshal. Fortunes of war. I do not have good news either. We tried nor-epinephrine on rabbits. They get up and hop away."

"Damn! What else have you tried?"

"This is not easy," Wolsky protested. "We have one autopsy. We do not have a prototype of the instrument we want to duplicate. If you could capture one of those weapons . . ."

"Capture!" Rogers gave a grim laugh. "When the Prl'lu show up we run. I run. Mordred runs.

We're helpless as ants waiting to be stepped on!"
He leaned across the desk. "I can't let my men
confront these creatures, Dr. Wolsky. When they
do, they die." He sank back. "What's your current
hypothesis?"

"Marshal, we have so little to go on—"

"Don't play games, Doc. You always have a
hypothesis no matter how weak you think it is."

Wolsky sighed. "Tanaka and I think it is cardiac
arrest. The heart stops."

"Why?"

"Somehow they confuse the nerve pulses that
control heart rhythm. Fibrillation results, followed immediately by unconsciousness and
death."

"Can you prevent it?"

"We can denervate the heart."

"Won't that kill you?"

"It makes the subject less capable of response to
exercise. A pacemaker would be better, but it
would have to be very sophisticated."

"Is it a big operation?"

"Ordinarily, but there's a drug which ac-
complishes the same thing for limited periods."

Rogers brightened. "We'd only have to take a
pill or an injection?"

"It is more complicated than that. The blocking
agent would have to be injected through the chest
wall directly into the heart."

"And if you survive that?" Rogers asked.

"Oh, the injection is nothing. But then you have
a slow heart, that does not respond to emergency
demands—and only maybe it works."

"And immunity to the death ray?"

"Only if it works."

"Tony, this has to be tested," Ruth began.

"I doubt if we have time. You two think of one experiment after another in logical progression. But we face two problems: the Prl'lu, and my ability to maintain control of that lilylivered council after these setbacks." He slumped, gazed into nothingness, and struggled to think while his friends waited. *My son! My son!*

He sat up. "I'll have to go to the council for authority. That means a delay until tomorrow. I'm going to trust Mordred's information. We'll hit the Prl'lu at Mount Erebus. Dr. Wolsky, you can supervise the heart treatment. Holcomb and I will find a squadron of volunteers. Ruth, try to find out how many airballs we have."

"Less than one hundred," she said. "The factories all converted to communications and other equipment. The airballs we do have were practically hand made. Factories are just getting tooled up."

He rubbed his forehead. "We'll use what we can get. Somebody get me an update on available airballs just before the council meeting, will you. Now I'd better call Major Dupre. She's got to think Dr. Wolsky is closer than ever to the secret of rejuvenation."

"Impossible! We have lost the equipment completely. I have nothing to work with. You insist I devote myself to this Prl'lu death ray—"

"I know, Doctor. But the only bait we have for those senile twits is the hope that our party controls the fountain of youth. I don't know how long I can keep up the deceit but I mean to squeeze as many votes out of it as possible."

"Politics!" Wolsky sneered.

"The art of the possible," Rogers defined. "If you want real disaster, just turn the government over to wellmeaning idealists. Besides, I have to defeat the Prl'lu to get your apparatus back."

The Prl'lu's face was impassive, eyes slitted. Mordred had learned to recognize this as a sign of emotion. "You would never have located the device without my intelligence network," he said.

"We are not deceived. You halfbreeds planned to use the lamrak device to bargain with us."

"Of course." Mordred tried to remain calm. "The value of my knowledge of the humans must be obvious by now."

"We should exterminate not only the humans, but also you."

Mordred folded his hands and remained silent. The room was large and, except for marble benches and a blocklike table, bare. The walls seemed of black glass flecked with tiny lights. Mordred had been in the room and thought there was a change in their pattern. His hands were cold. That was a sign of *his* emotion. Dealing with the Prl'lu was no different from negotiating with Han or human, he assured himself. A colossal arrogance made them, if anything, easier to manipulate. "I would like to volunteer my own forces to destroy their command center," Mordred said.

"How?"

"My spies have infiltrated. Timing is crucial, but I have a plan to draw off their air forces. To penetrate the final defenses I will need the karnak ray. The Citadel is impregnable to ordinary weapons."

The Prl'lu considered. "This will be your last

chance to prove yourself useful. Fail and you will die with the rest of your worthless race."

"I have no fear of failure."

"That is surprising, considering your accomplishments to date."

Mordred suppressed his rage. "I inherited an empire in ruins, with neither weapons nor the will to fight. What I have done will be remembered."

"The Han were not bred for military operations. Their role was purely supportive."

"The Han underestimated the human potential," Mordred admitted. "I will not repeat the previous emperor's mistake."

"I should hope not, considering your heritage."

Mordred did not reply to this insult.

The Prl'lu studied him from expressionless eyes. Finally he spoke again. "We will send one ship with karnak death ray apparatus. You will scout an opening for the attack. You will respond for any failure. You have ten days. You may go."

Mordred bowed and backed out of the room. As he walked the corridors under Antarctica back to his ship the tension refused to dissolve. I have only to be sure of my timing, he thought. His agent inside the Citadel would guarantee that. He would yet live to see the Prl'lu humbled and his human enemies destroyed.

"Betide me death, betide me life," said the king, "Now I see him yonder alone he shall never escape my hands, for at a better vantage shall I never have him."

"God speed you well," said Sir Bedivere.

Then the king gat his spear in both hands, and he ran

toward Sir Mordred, crying "Traitor, now is thy death day come."

And when Sir Mordred heard King Arthur, he ran unto him with his sword drawn in his hand. And then King Arthur smote Sir Mordred under the shield with a foiss of his spear throughout the body more than a fathom. And when Sir. Mordred felt he had his death's wound, he thrust himself, with the last might that he had, up to the bur of King Arthur's spear. And right so he smote the king with his sword holden in both hands, on the side of the head, that the sword did pierce the helmet and the brain pan. And therewith Sir Mordred fell stark dead to the earth. And the noble Arthur fell in a swoon and lay senseless.

Anthony Rogers snapped off the vidscreen and punched a button for the recording to be returned to archives. He looked up at the big sunfilled reading room of the university library.

"I wonder," he said to himself, "why Arthur did not use his great magical sword Excalibur in the last and greatest battle of his life." But he thought he knew. Though it may sometimes be necessary—even desirable—no father really wants to kill his son.

XII

———◆—◆◆◆—◆———

Rogers leaned over the vidplate in the belly of the RB-25. Six days of wild scramble and improvisation lay behind. Antarctica lay ahead. In the next twenty four hours he would conquer or be conquered by the Prl'lu.

Crowded into the ship's central com room were six consoles for airball control. These weapons were round projectiles less than a meter in diameter inertron-balanced to zero weight, and propelled by small jets. Each had an ultra beam eye through which the operator could direct it from kilometers away. Each ball carried *dis* and *rep* rays, projectiles, gas, and self-destruct charges.

But though the airballs had been crucial to American victory in the War of Liberation, they had disadvantages. Their controllable range was only a thousand kilometers, which meant the air armada had to penetrate well into Antarctica before they could be launched. Also, though efforts had been made to build more, most of these airballs were left over from the previous Han war, and were showing their age.

The airballs' greatest weakness of all was that they needed a human controller: if something happened to the human his twenty airballs drifted with the perfect apathy of undirected machines. And machines never care. This was why Rogers had three identical control setups: one aboard the RB-25 in the main strike force, one with a smaller force which was to land near the pole and dig in with *dis*, and a third backup console aboard a squadron of airships with *dis* adjusted to bore in under the ice of the Ross Sea's frigid waters.

The weapons themselves were carried by Strike Force Group Nine, with Rogers in command. The ground station would land from unarmed transports accompanied by fighter escort. Strike Group Six would then head in toward Mount Erebus under the newly promoted Captain Holcomb.

Strike Group Three covered Rogers' left: ten one-man rockets manned by volunteers. Though he thought it bad for morale, Rogers could not stop the young men and women from privately calling themselves the Suicide Club.

Rogers' twelve-ship command was conventionally armed and included the RB-25, America's only "new generation" dreadnaught. His ace in the hole was the undersea squadron, Strike Group Twelve: four ships specially equipped to turn them into ultron-armored submarines running on *dis*—powered water jets.

Knowing the enemy had penetrated his ultraphone network. Rogers maintained total silence from the time the fleet launched from three sites in North America and one in Peru. He studied the screen. For hours the ocean had been a jumble of melted and refrozen ice. The continent

was practically bare but even Prl'lu could not
warm the whole antarctic zone: the conflict between a warm center surrounded by frigid ocean
promised some interesting weather.

There was, as yet, no sign of life. Rock steamed
as they reached land. Ground water was collect-
ing in streams and lakes.

The fleet sped on, toward its fate.

Strike Group Six hovered while the two transports dissed themselves into polar rock. When the
ships were out of sight Holcomb sighed his relief.
His command was scattered in a wide crescent to
cover the ground operation. Clouds were gathering over the wet rocky peaks of Antarctica. Holcomb could see infrantry jumping from rock to
rock as they fanned across the hills. A few had
already begun digging in with portable dis. Their
uniforms were dark to blend with the wet rock
and they were visible only when they belted in
long arcs.

Yolanda Entallador was one of those jumping
black dots on that forebidding landscape. He
dipped a wing in salute and headed for his next
station, glancing at the chronometer. Ahead of
schedule. Tony's plan was working so far. Now
where the hell were the Prl'lu? "Know soon," he
muttered.

"Pardon, sir?" his copilot asked.

"Nothing. Squadron in formation?"

"Perfect, sir. I wonder where the enemy is."

"So do I."

Strike Group Nine released airballs into the sky
just beyond 80°S. One exploded, putting another

dozen out of action. Controllers uttered ingenious blasphemies and jockeyed their remaining weapons into the clouds, fighting crosswinds with jets. On Rogers' scope each airball was an orange dot. Blue represented the dozen ships of his personal command: other squadrons, other colors. He glanced at the chronometer. "Polar attack force should be dug in by now," he said. "Release control on the tenth series."

"Control off, sir." They watched the scopes for an anxious moment, then the airballs made a sweep of the fleet and resumed position.

"They've got alternate control working," Rogers said. "Series onc, attack."

"Aye, sir." Ten airballs disappeared over the horizon. Ground and sky in rapid motion appeared on the vidscreens. Major Twitchell, captain of the RB-25, called from his control room in the top of the dumbbell craft. "Nothing in sight, Marshal. Request permission to ultrascope max range."

"Go ahead. If they can't pick up airball control frequencies they're still in bed."

"Very good, sir."

"No ship-to-ship ultraphone," Rogers cautioned. "Not until we engage."

The airballs were now producing contrails. Behind them came the fleet. Doubt began to grow in Rogers. Had Mordred sent him and his troops to the far end of the earth on a wild goose chase?

Lu-An had said, "I do not know what has happened between my uncle and the Prl'lu, but I believe the information he gave you was correct—at least to the best of his knowledge." She had sat on the otherside of the desk. The tiny scar where a transmitter had been removed was hidden by the hair over her left ear. A guard stood impassive behind her.

"It's tempting to believe," Rogers had replied. "Probably thinks the Prl'lu will destroy us for him."

"He undoubtedly hopes his enemies will destroy each other," the Han girl agreed. "But if that is his intent, then he will give you the best intelligence and throw you directly at them. The Prl'lu are the superior force." She fell silent. Then, in a whisper, "He means your destruction. Do not go."

"Contact!" Rogers snapped back to the present. Airballs showed trap doors in the rock flipping open, squat ray projectors glinting sinister in the sun. *Dis* swept them, but the airballs jetted on.

"First stroke," Rogers said. "Break silence."

"Missiles away, sir," the gunnery officer reported as two dozen rockets soared.

"Get your airballs out of the way!" Rogers ordered, "Instruments, did you get a report?"

A comtech held up a tape.

"Relay that off to Niagra," Rogers snapped. Ahead of them the black hills flared with atomic fire.

"Message away, sir," the comtech called.

Rogers had taken one airball out of combat to carry a bunch of Dr. Tanaka's instruments. Now at least the information would reach the scientist. "Get me airball surveillance of the target area. Patch me into the command net to units Six and Three."

"Scope four, sir." The airball circled over still molten rock where the enemy ray battery had been. He glanced at the other scopes. "Any contact?'' he asked. "Captain Holcomb?"

Four red dots flashed at the edge of the scope.

"Ultrabeam contact," Holcomb's calm voice said. "Approaching our position at fourteen hundred kilometers per hour. I am attacking."

"God go with you." 1400 kph was faster than the bullets Rogers had fired in the war of his own era. He turned to his staff. "Get an airball screen to intercept those Prl'lu. Our own screen to advance on schedule. Group Three report."

"No contact, sir."

"I have a back plot on the attacker, sir," a computer tech called. "The azimuth passes right over Mount Erebus."

"That's it, then," Rogers sighed.

"Contact," said an airball controller. "Scope two." The advancing sphere had found enemy ships: dead black finned slivers, white contrails following like a bad reputation.

"What've you got in range?"

"Two balls, sir. Oops! One ball."

"Close and engage if you can," Rogers said. Holcomb's atomics exploded among the on rushing Prl'lu. One red dot on Rogers' screen went out. The other three proceeded on course. The airball kept them in sight as they crossed paths with the Americans. The black ships swept through a holocaust of explosive missiles and crisscrossing dis beams at incredible speed. Enemy fire burst among Holcomb's squadron. American rep beams caught one of the attackers. The Prl'lu ship twisted, burned a hole in the rock, and plunged into it. The other two were already over the horizon.

"Get your airball in the hole after that ship,"

Rogers ordered. "What's your armament?"

"*Dis* and high explosive, sir."

"Hit him if you can. The rest of you get airball section two over there. Group Six report."

There was an instant of delay and Rogers' heart sank. On the screen the American ships hung motionless as the airball rushed toward them. The ball angled down the *dis* ray hole. Its eye saw nothing but smooth fused rock walls.

Holcomb's voice came on and relief rippled through the com room. But his news was not good. "Four ships do not respond and are presumed lost. Two others damaged but still flying. The enemy has withdrawn toward Ground Group Six. Permission to pursue?"

"Stay on course," Rogers said. "Leave one of your cripples to deal with the downed Prl'lu if it reappears." He knew what was on Holcomb's mind. The Prl'lu were headed right for Entallador's infantry.

Rogers' right flank was decimated, but his attack was closing in on the Prl'lu stronghold. No new dots appeared on the screen.

"Erebus in sight, sir." A towering, smoking mountain appeared before the advancing airballs.

"Active again," Rogers commented. "That volcano was supposed to be extinct."

"Ground Six reports enemy contact," a tech interrupted.

"Aknol," Rogers said. "Release airballs eight and nine to their control."

"Look at that!" one airball controller cried. Across the sky a wall of pale blue fire flared like some insane borealis.

"*Dis* ray barrier," Rogers said. "Take the balls through it."

Techs bent to their screens. As the first airball through the screen went blank. They switched to a ball not yet within the shield. Vidplates showed only the pale *dis* barrier rising from rocky ground up out of sight.

"Lost control," a tech called.

"Try again," Rogers said. Once more the screen went blank as the ball entered the wall of *dis*.

"It doesn't disintegrate," one tech reported. "We were watching with the other balls. It entered the *dis*, then became indistinct."

The tech who had been controlling the first ball worked controls. "Doesn't respond," she said. "I've tried bringing it back."

"The rest of you stay out of it," Rogers directed. "See if you can go over the top. Those rays are usually a couple of kilometers high."

He turned to the big screen. "Where're all those Prl'lu?"

"They swept out past the ground base and headed toward the Weddell Sea."

"Group Six?"

"They drew a lot of fire. The surface forces were all wiped out. Underground units are still functional. They've still got twenty six airballs under their control. They're fanning out."

"Aknol. Keep me posted. Strike Group Nine?"

"No contact, sir."

"Tell him to move into final assault position," Rogers ordered. "I may need him in a hurry. What's with the airballs?"

"You were right, sir," a tech said. "I got one

over the top at two kilometers. But at that height all you can see is smoke. Soon as I dropped I lost control and my screen blanked out."

"Aknol," Rogers said. He thought a moment. "How big is that ring of dis? Can we encircle it?"

"Message from Niagra, sir."

"Let's have it."

The Prl'lu were coming back over the pole. He wondered how Entallador's airball controllers were doing.

"Wolsky and Tanaka report data received are consistent with cardiac arrest hypothesis," the comtech reported.

"Relay that to Strike Group Three," Rogers said.

"Got it, Marshal," the group leader spoke up, "But what does it mean?"

"These scientific types will never give you a sure thing," Rogers replied. "The experiment shows that you guys are immune but they want to hedge their bets."

"Marshal," the controller called, "We've got the ray barrier encircled. "It's five kilometers across. Encloses the whole mountain. No openings."

Rogers studied the screen as she flipped from one eye to another. American ships had now come into range of the ray barrier and hovered as the airballs circled it. "Should be penetrable with inertron missiles," Rogers mused. "See if you can shoot an air ball straight through—out the other side."

"Aye, sir."

"Enemy coming over the pole, sir," another tech reported. These were the two who had attacked Holcomb's group.

"Sections Five and Six intercept," Rogers said. "Report from Ground Six?"

"Alive but lost their airballs. Says the ships were drawn off at the last minute."

Rogers released a breath. "Came after us," he said. "We must be doing something right."

"Opening in the barrier," a tech called. Rogers swung to the scope. A gap had appeared in the pale wall of dis. Suspended in it were six dark finned shapes.

"Missiles away!" the gunnery officer called.

"Get the balls out of there!" Rogers warned. The gunnery officer was using atomics. Every ship in the squadron had fired on his command. A fireball ten kilometers across pushed against the ray barrier. The dis absorbed most of the force, fueling a hurricane thousands of miles away with the displaced energy. Six airballs disappeared. Rogers ordered a wider formation as the Prl'lu ships began emerging from the holocaust. They advanced behind a screen of wide angle dis.

"Airballs aloft!" Rogers ordered. "Attack from above or below. Get around the barrier or penetrate it!"

The Prl'lu were flying close formation, dis fanning to negate the missiles that rained on them. They drove straight for the center of the American fleet. Some rockets penetrated ray screens but failed to penetrate armor. Slowly, the Americans withdrew.

"I've got an airball out the other side and over the ocean," a controller called.

"Airball penetration of the air fleet," another reported. "but I can't get close enough to damage them. They keep repping me back out."

"Their left flank screen looks weak. Concentrate airball attack there. Rocket batteries to distract them as much as possible. And keep back: we may be out of range."

"Prl'lu approaching from the rear, sir." Rogers had been watching the approach on his scope. Now he was caught between two forces.

"Take them under fire with the third division," he ordered. "the rest of the squadron continue on present target. Group Six, follow and engage. Groups Three and Twelve, proceed with attack."

While the barrage slowed the enemy, there was no hint that it had inflicted any damage. So far, the Prl'lu had not responded with death rays. Meanwhile, airball after airball detonated against the left flank of the black ships. And finally one ship faltered and began to lose altitude. As it did so, the ray barrier began to fail, making the other ships more susceptible to missiles.

"Get dis ray airballs in there with chemical shells," Rogers ordered. The embattled fleets had drifted closer and now the two ships coming up from the south crossed behind his at incredible velocity. For an instant it seemed as if nothing had happened. Then missile fire on the attacking Prl'lu died down to an occasional explosion.

"Get a report," Rogers ordered. "Strike Group Three, enemy at high speed crossing your vector. Get 'em!"

"Aye, sir." The Suicide Squadron moved out.

"Eight ships do not respond, sir." The comtech's voice was husky. "All units holding their last course."

"Ultra probe a couple." Rogers bent over the scope. The remaining four Prl'lu bore down on his

squadron. They had death rayed all but his first
rank, leaving only the RB-25 and three scout craft
under his direct command. He did not want to
abandon the other eight ships until he knew all
his troops were dead. To board them in mid-
battle was out of the question. To ultrabeam each
one would take too long. No time to think: time
only to act!

"Fan out and flank attackers. RB-25 will continue to withdraw. How many airballs left?"

"Sixteen, sir."

"Not enough." Faintly, through com center's
ultraphones, he could hear Strike Group Three as
it sighted the enemy and maneuvered to close.
Holcomb's three ships appeared over the horizon,
one trailing.

"Hold off the airballs. We'll need them for the
mountain. Give them everything else we've got!"

It was not enough. *Dis* churned a rock and water
whirlpool before the oncoming ships, but these
were not *rep* ray suspended. They flew over the
dissolving ground with impunity. Inertron
shielded missiles reached them, but their incredible armor plate absorbed the continued battering.
They moved slowly, shields up: nothing not made
of inertron touched them.

"Chemical shells and *dis*," Rogers ordered.
"Break that barrier!"

The gunnery officer turned to his com line. Two
hammer blows staggered the ship, throwing Rogers to the deck. On the forward scope they saw
the Prl'lu ships rise and sweep over them. The
RB-25 was caught in a bath of *dis*. Powerful *rep*
slammed against the upper armor, pushing the
ship toward the rocks.

"Captain Twitchell!" There was no reply. Rogers leaped upward to topside control. The force of the attack had smashed in the ultron canopy. The ship's captain and copilot were dead. Rogers dropped back to the com cabin. The RB-25 was plunging.

"Rep rays!" Rogers called to the gunnery officer. "Straight down, full power!"

Despite the gunner's quick response, the RB-25 hit the ground hard. Three of the black Prl'lu were hovering above while a fourth ship had descended to land beside her; black armored figures boiled out and began raying the armor on the forward sphere.

"Got 'em!" a voice suddenly cried on the ultraphone. "It works. We're immune!" Strike Group Three continued to exult as they moved into position around the ray-shielded Mount Erebus.

"Can we burn those guys off our hull?" Rogers asked the gunnery officer."

"No chance, sir. They're in too close."

Rogers glanced around the com room. "Your captain's dead," he said. "You're in charge. I'll take three men. Break out full armor and we'll go forward to repel boarders."

As he clapped on his helmet Rogers felt the shudder as two sets of ray batteries struggled to control the battleship's position. So far, he thought, no death ray attack. These ships must not have it. He led three techs down the central shaft to the lowest levels.

Armor plate was buckling. Whatever the Prl'lu had was an order of magnitude more powerful than any Han weapon; inertron and ultron were

not impenetrable after all. The weakened hull
burst inward. He jumped aside as dis roared. The
ship's interior was not made of inertron. Equipment, bulkheads, and instruments vanished. The
hole to the opposite side of the hull filled with
flying scrap as the power went. Rogers flicked on
his helmet light just as the first invader leaped in.
He poured rocket shells and dis into the Prl'lu.
The next soldier shot in, hitting the farther side of
the hull and bouncing back before the Americans
could swing their weapons. As dis swept back
and forth, annihilating everything except an occasional ultron-shielded cable Rogers glanced up.
It was only three levels up to com control.

The second Prl'lu had a rodlike weapon in his
hand. He aimed it and the armored trooper next to
Rogers slumped; Death rays came in several sizes.
He dived into tackle, somehow he got both hands
on the creature's arm. The Prl'lu lifted him off the
deck and flung him from side to side as they
struggled for the weapon. The other two rushed to
Rogers' aid. One came into the path of the invisible death ray. The Prl'lu slammed the other
against the hull.

The Prl'lu's superhuman strength would have
made short work of Rogers had not the RB-25
suddenly lurched into the air. The Suicide Squadron had knocked out the Prl'lu ships holding the
RB-25 to earth, and as the American ship shot
skyward on unopposed rep it rolled; Rogers and
his opponent fell through the breach in the side of
the ship. They toppled into space.

As they fell, for a moment Rogers could see his
opponent's dark face. He saw the thin mouth
open. Then they were torn apart and he was spin-

ning earthward with terrible speed, pressed down by the rep beams of his own ship. Desperately, he belted and with stuttering blasts managed to jet free. He watched as the Prl'lu slammed into the earth. The crippled RB-25, forward compartment gutted, flew off into the sky. "Hey," Rogers yelled. "Somebody pick me up!"

XIII

The commander of the Suicide Club took him aboard. They had three ships destroyed and two crippled. Rogers' command group had been wiped out. The RB-25, pride of the American force, was now a useless hulk rising toward the stratosphere. As Rogers crawled into the hovering scout he had little to be happy about. The cylinder of *dis* about the Prl'lu base remained unbreached.

"Welcome aboard, sir." The pilot slid over to make room. "Glad to see you alive."

"It beats the alternatives," Rogers said glumly. "How did you get rid of the rest of the Prl'lu?"

"By accepting 85% casualties," the pilot replied. "After that it was easy."

"How many ships have we got left?"

"Holcomb has three operational and three damaged. I have four left in good shape. Ground Six is dug in but they report surface vehicles to their east."

Rogers punched the ultrabeam. "Marshal Rogers here. Anybody got bandits in sight? Ground Six, what's your situ? Are you under attack?"

"Negative." "Negative." reported the two air units. "Negative aircraft, sir," from Ground Six. "Unknown number of ground vehicles approaching. Request rocket support or airball control."

"How many airballs on your scopes now?" With the RB-25 out of action and Strike Group Three still unrevealed, the ground control unit was the only one in contact.

"Twelve."

"Transfer two more to your own sector," Rogers ordered. "Take one of the others up close to the *dis* ray wall. Patch me direct to the controller."

"Here, sir," said a new voice. While Rogers gave instructions his pilot put the little ship in position over the ocean fifty kilometers from the tower of blue fire.

"Tony," said Holcomb's voice, "Let us go to the support of Ground Six."

Rogers knew what that request meant to the young officer and what it cost him to break regulations and ask it. "Denied," he said. "One job at a time."

Airball penetration of the *dis* barrier was possible. No more enemy ships emerged. But missiles sent through the wall were lost to control while inside.

"Angle high," Rogers directed. The distant controller launched an airball set to detonate on contact with anything material. The airball disappeared. Nothing happened.

"G-6 command, we are under attack by *dis* rays and armored troops."

"Strike Group Twleve," Rogers called. "Code one eighty nine. Break silence."

"Here Marshal," came the immediate reply "We're waiting for—" The voice broke off, came on again. "We've been monitoring the airball attack. That last one showed something before it blacked out."

"Take control of the airballs while G-6 is under attack. Keep up the pressure: we're beginning to wear them down." To wear down Prl'lu, Rogers thought, was like honing a sword with a cantaloupe. But he knew the airballs were penetrating the *dis* rays, probably going off inside the wall. Four more disappeared before another report came from operator twelve.

"Clear picture before detonation that time, sir. An installation at the bottom of the crater. They've taken hits."

"Keep at them," Rogers ordered. Unfortunately, the submarine could control only one airball at a time. He needed G-6 controllers but voices on the ultraphone told him that Entallador's troops were fighting for their lives.

"Save your last airball, twelve. Send it in on a flat trajectory."

"Got it! Clear view of the ground. Oops—they hit me. Screen's blank again. Ball still responds. I'm going to smash her straight down!"

Rogers turned to the pilot beside him. "Commander," he said, "We'll take your squadron in. The Prl'lu device for knocking out our instrumentation seems to be neutralized."

"Aye, sir." The pilot snapped out his orders. The four ships zoomed in at the ray wall, penetrated. Beneath, the crater opened. Machinery, pumps, massive conduits covered the crater bottom except where airballs had cleared bare

patches. One of the American ships reeled,
plunged, smashed against the crater wall.

"Dis!" Rogers saw the projectors. "Pick off that
thing on the far wall." The ship swerved, missiles
flew as the group concentrated its fire on the sus-
picious installation. There was no return fire from
the Prl'lu. The building blew up; the ray wall
remained. The commander kept tight formation
as they swept around the periphery of the crater,
knocking off one building after another. Finally
the barrier dissolved. Holcomb's three ships still
circled the mountain outside.

"Cover us," Rogers ordered. "We're going to
land."

Machinery dwarfed the ships. Tiny armored
figures belted in open formation, leaving one man
to guard each ship. Automatic defense devices
threw dis and rep rays but no Prl-lu appeared.

"Have we wiped them out?" Rogers asked. The
crater was five kilometers across and full of
ruined machinery. It could take forever to search
it.

"Tunnel, sir," called one of the exploring
group.

"Any more enemy ships?"

"None, sir," Holcomb replied.

"I find it hard to believe that the enemy would
abandon his base in an all-or-nothing frontal assault," Rogers grumbled. The Prl'lu must be waiting somewhere. "Group Three pilots hold up
there and take defensive positions. Holcomb,
bring your ships down inside and have one man
from each ship dismount."

"All my ships, sir?"

"All twelve." Rogers and Holcomb both knew he did not have that many. The three ships landed and one man from each of their two-man crews belted out. Still nothing happened.

"What now, sir?"

"Mill around a little. Some of you land and hide in the shadows. Group Twelve, remain ready."

"Here they come!" Trapdoors opened and dark aircraft emerged into the crater. These were not warships, but big open platforms on rep rays manned by troops in the open who were running across the decks. Hasty conversions, Rogers supposed. Dis began pouring down on the Americans. "Group Twelve, jet in!"

The Prl'lu installations were mostly unshielded. Dis left great furrows in the bare rock. Also exposed was a maze of tunnels. A dis ray caught Rogers. The building he was standing on vanished and he began to fall gently toward the blasted rock. The ray passed on and he gasped as returning air tried to flatten his empty lungs.

Strike Group Twelve's four ships appeared. Holcomb's pilots took to the air. The Prl'lu vehicles were tossed in a crossfire of exploding missiles and dis. Two were blown to bits in the first exchange. Another was forced down with rep rays just in front of Rogers. As he watched the enemy craft was carved by dis. A handful of armorclad fighters flew from the doomed vehicle, three in his direction. He cut at the swooping figures but his hand-held dis had no effect. As they flashed closer he belted high and pulled a rodlike object from his belt. As the Prl'lu approached he aimed and fingered the button. They stopped firing. One weapon tumbled to the rock below. Black armored figures passed beneath him and slammed into the crater wall.

"Really works," he grunted. "Won't Wolsky be delighted if I live to get it to him!"

The Suicide Club was belting after survivors of the destroyed Prl'lu vehicles.

"Holcomb," he called, "take your squadron to support Ground Six. Situation's under control here."

Entallador's surviving Peruvians had done their job and Holcomb's arrival, while welcome, was no rescue. Airlifted into the Mount Erebus crater, they located several items of interest. The equipment from the rejuvenation chamber had been found intact. This alone would justify Rogers' casualties to the council. Machinery and conduits running in all directions were probably the means by which the Prl'lu had melted the polar cap and inundated their enemies. Had American civilization not within the last two centuries been all but destroyed by catastrophe and invasion, Rogers mused, this stratagem might well have ended the war. But American industry was still spread wide through the wilderness and mountains where it had hidden from the Han.

"I wonder what Lu-An would make of all this," he said to Holcomb as they stood on a catwalk looking down into a pit filled with ten-meter-wide-tubes that pierced the tectonic plate.

"We've found why the place is so deserted," Holcomb said.

The domed chamber was enormous. Entallador

and several of his people, including the lovely
Yolanda, maintained an uneasy guard at the en-
tryway, fingering their weapons. Inside the floor
rose slightly toward the far wall so that tier upon
tier of transparent capsules could be seen. Each
capsule was three meters long and had its own
metal base. Only a few close to the door were open
and empty. Each of the remaining thousand of
capsules contained a nude motionless figure.

Rogers walked between rows of sleepers,
studied the handful of empty capsules. "Must
have needed the revivification apparatus after
all," he said. "And if this handful nearly wiped us
out, what happens if they all wake up?"

"Now, before it is too late, Marshal," Entallador
insisted. "One at a time we open these capsules
and use *dis*."

Rogers remembered the problems Wolsky had
had trying to open his and General Gordon's capsules. "I think maybe we'd have better luck
slowly cutting down on the power supply," he
guessed. "That might start deterioration before
they were sufficiently awakened to shift for themselves. But we'll have to wait for Dr. Wolsky's
opinion."

"Urgent," a comtech said. "Urgent for Marshal
Rogers from Wyoming Base."

The ship came in low over the forest; the occupants of the upper levels of the Citadel were dead
before they knew they were under attack. Han in
bright red jackets with three Prl'lu in command
landed and hit the walls with explosives and a
giant *dis* projector. Troops rushed up from under-

ground to defend the breach were mown down in swathes by the Prl'lu death ray.

Lu-An heard a warning shout, then the steel door to her cell dissolved. Rough hands hurried her to the surface and out where rep ray ships could pick them up. The raid took less than an hour. In the confusion Rogers' expeditionary force had not been notified; it was only after he got the message that the Wyoming space port had been attacked that he discovered communication with Niagra was still down.

"Well, raise me somebody!" he raged.

"I can get you TexArk field, sir." The tech's voice was tense but level.

ComTex told him that most of Niagra had been wiped out, but that somebody was still in control. The Wyoming base raid had just been reported to them. "We assume, sir, that they have captured the *Wilma Deering.*"

Rogers wondered how they could have made off with a ship that was possibly years from completion the last time he had inspected. What else was going on without his knowledge? "Have you got a contact there?" he asked. "Can you put me through?" He turned to his aides. "Holcomb, get this handgun death ray to Wolsky and Harris at the university. We need a long range model and we need a shield." What he needed was a miracle.

"Entallador remains in command here. Suicide Squadron and Group Twelve will support him—what's left of them. I'll take one of Group Six's ships and a pilot and fly to Wyoming. No, Holcomb, I'll go in the larger ship so I can look important. Meanwhile, you *get through with that death ray.*" He turned back to the long range ultra beam operator. "Confirmed? Aknol and thank you. Beam off."

He turned to the others. "Mordred has the *Wilma Deering*. That just about makes my day."

XIV

———◆—◆◆—◆———

A handful of troops ranged the echoing corridors of the Citadel. Rogers' office was intact. In it Major Dupre and Colonel Watson had been waiting; they were the ranking survirors.

A new council should be formed but there wasn't time; Rogers didn't want to wait. He wanted action!

"I know it's illogical; I was off duty," Major Dupre said. "But I feel guilty. I should have died with the others."

He took her by the shoulders. "What we must do—those of us who are still alive—is to consolidate our control of the Prl'lu installation in Antarctica. Then we can run down Mordred." He paced while the others watched. "How did he get the Prl'lu to give him the death ray? They were as much his enemies as we were."

"The same way he got us to send all our ships to the South Pole," Colonel Watson said. "He promised what we all wanted most—a quick clean shot at the enemy."

"Yes," Rogers agreed. "It was a near thing; we nearly wiped each other out, just as he hoped we would—but where is he now?"

"No trace," Major Dupre reported. "We've got as many commercial airships out looking as we can spare, and we've contacted local gangs all over the world."

"Keep at it," Rogers said. "The Han have shielded bases that do not yield to ultrabeam probe but we've got to keep trying."

"It would help if we could get the ships back from the South Pole," Watson said.

"Not a chance. That's where he'll strike next."

"It's as if he vanished off the face of the earth."

Rogers slammed his fist into his desk top. "But he did! The *Wilma Deering* is a space ship!" He dialed a comtech, who looked haggard and sleepy. All Citadel personnel were on double and triple duty. "Priority red," Rogers said. "Get me Dr. Harris or Dr. Wolsky at the university."

"Aknol, sir. Dr. Harris has a call in for you. We delayed it, knowing you were in conference."

Ruth listened while Rogers outlined his problem. "I also want to know if Holcomb got to Wolsky with the gadget I sent him and if so how he's doing. It's good to see you," he added.

"It's good to see you too, Tony." She brushed back her hair. "Holcomb is here and Wolsky is delighted with your gift. A couple of physicists are taking it apart. Your other problem is more difficult. There's not much real astromony being done these days. I'll call you back."

It was hours before Ruth Harris made that call. In the meantime the council survivors toiled over reports and grim decisions. With the American air force destroyed or tied down in Antarctica, how many ships should be on general duty? How many searching for the *Wilma Deering?* How many in reserve? There were not enough ships to do any one of the three jobs properly. Tired orderlies brought food and coffee. Finally Ruth Harris called.

"I've located an astronomer—Dr. Mamboya, this is Marshal Rogers."

The black face of the astronomer appeared on the vidscreen. Rogers explained what he wanted to know. When the African understood his smile was bleak. "I have, of course, colleagues I can contact all over the world, but global surveillance is impossible."

"Why is that, Doctor?" Rogers asked.

"Facilities, funds, and manpower for astronomy have never been high priority items in your budget, Marshal."

"Dr. Mamboya, the importance of astronomy had just become glaringly apparent," Rogers said. "Assuming humans survive, and assuming I survive, your specialty will very soon find its place in a greatly augmented sun, but for now we must do what we can with what we have."

"Very good, sir," the African said after this was translated. "Now, if I understand, you do not want observers around the world to know exactly what it is they are looking for so I'll tell my friends a new comet has been reported, but that the report is unreliable, with position and orbit unknown. But I must have an approximate location if this report is to be believable."

"Somewhere over North America the night of—" Rogers looked at his aides. "Early morning,

probably the eighteenth. I would expect a stable
orbit with respect to the earth's surface but that
may not be true."

"Most assuredly not true if you speak of com-
ets," the astronomer said. He shrugged. "I'll do
what I can."

Twenty four hours passed without news. What
was Mordred doing? Surely he would strike now
while the American forces were depleted. Did he
have problems of his own? What shape was the
Wilma Deering in? Surely the space ship had not
been finished. If it had been, Rogers would have
found a way to use it against the Han and the
Prl'lu. But maybe Mordred was only suffering
from the same kind of personnel shortage that
plagued Rogers' every move.

When Captain Holcomb tired of watching
physicists fool with the captured death ray he
suddenly realized he was under no compulsion to
remain; he flew to Niagra with Ruth Harris. "I
wish you hadn't come," Rogers greeted her. "No
military installation is safe—least of all this one."

"I keep wondering if I'll ever see you again.
This whole thing has happened so fast." Which
was her oblique way of saying he was twenty five
and she was forty.

He folded her in his arms and stroked her hair.
"Perhaps we'll find Mordred soon."

"Are you glad to see me?"

"Of course. I need your help and advice."

She had to be satisfied with that.

Next day Holcomb called from the university.
"The electronics boys and girls say the death ray's
no big problem once you see one. They're build-

ing one on board the *Eagle*. It's big and awkward, but it works. We tried it on a cageful of rats at two kilometers. It doesn't kill plants, by the way and there seems to be an exponential increment in energy requirements with distance. That may be solved when they figure out how to focus it."

"Let us hope they're right about that," Rogers said. "When the ship's ready, fly here."

"Aknol."

The next message was relayed from Dr. Mamboya. A comtech read off the celestial coordinates. "It's a comet hunter one jump ahead of the flood in Sas-Toon. He has only a small telescope but he says it's a ship and not a comet. He's sure it's Martians."

"They might be easier to deal with," Rogers said.

"Urgent, sir," another tech cut in. "Message from Prince Mordred."

"About time," Rogers growled.

Mordred was pale and gaunt. Dark eyes held a manic gleam.

"So good of you to call," Rogers greeted. "We were about to send out a search party."

"By now you have probably discovered that I hang over your planet, positioned to bomb or ray any portion. Now that, with my aid, you've vanquished the Prl'lu, you may think to challenge the might of the Han. Do not be deceived. Lest you disbelieve, I will destroy the Sierra Nevada north of the drowned city of Fisco and let the rising ocean into the western desert. After that my bombs will fall elsewhere.

"Mark you, worms of Earth, that the Americans provided me with this power of destruction. Masses of Asia, Africa, and Europe, this is the weapon the American Rogers built in his secret base. You would never have known without my intervention. Now watch while I turn it on its creators."

Rogers groaned and turned to Major Dupre. "Try to get the chief bosses of as many confederations as possible on the ultraphone. We'll issue a rebuttal as soon as this lunatic stops raving." He paused, watching the dark visage on the screen. Was there really a resemblance to himself? "Be sure the comtechs are tracking this," he added.

Mordred continued, "The Han Empire is inclined, at least for now, to be lenient. To all but the Americans and their genocidal leader, Anthony Rogers."

"Got a track," Dupre whispered. "He's sending from the ship alright."

Major Dupre's ultraphone lit up and she answered. "Marshal," she said, "Mordred's done it: a refugee camp in the western mountains was vaporized. Reno reports an earthquake."

Mordred interrupted his diatribe to display the disc of Earth as seen from the *Wilma Deering*. Night was creeping over the eastern seaboard of North America but beyond the inundated central plains the mountains were clear beneath a light scatter of clouds. At the edge of the land, above the Pacific blue a tiny round black cloud was forming, rising and expanding, shot now with lurid orange light. "See the first stroke of Han vengeance! The death of a continent! Nothing can save you but the mercy of the Han—which is earned by obedience. From this position I observe all—and can destroy all. The war-technology of the Prl'lu at my command. Nothing can approach my orbiting command post. We have only to push away your slowflying bombs with the rep rays so conveniently provided by the American war-lords."

He can, Rogers knew. Direct assault was never going to work. How long could he stay up there before his men started running out of water and air? How long to turn Earth into radioactive waste? How many bombs did he actually have? Rogers did not for a moment believe the destruction would end when North America was wiped out. That was just a minor ploy to keep Earth squabbling instead of organizing against Mordred. Was there any way Rogers could get up there? Could he trade himself for a planet? He triggered his ultraphone. "When Captain Holcomb arrives, get him to my office immediately."

"Tony," Ruth Harris's eyes were still on the vidscreen where Mordred was pointing out his next target. "Tony," she repeated, "A ship in orbit is held there by gravitation."

Rogers whistled. "You're right. He can't orbit a weightless ship! Either he's dropped some of his inertron shielding or it wasn't all installed yet. Now if we could just get a dis ray on him!"

Holcomb entered. "Reporting as ordered, sir."

"Just in time! Major Dupre, continue monitoring Mordred's broadcast. We'll reply when he finishes." Rogers leaped from behind the desk and they belted out of the Citadel to the hovering Eagle.

The death-ray machine had been installed across the starboard side of the ship, and a long cylindrical gas tank had been strapped on the port side, destroying the rocket's streamlined symmetry. A series of brass tubes and knobs were welded to the outside of the hull and linked by a shielded cable. "Ugly as homemade sin," Rogers commented.

"Also interferes with opening the canopy," Holcomb said. They squeezed in one at a time and Holcomb pointed out the new weapon's controls. The ultraphone was on and Mordred's face filled the screen. He was still talking. Other screens showed the Citadel below and flight charts for the northern hemisphere.

"How's your air supply?" Rogers asked.

"Full. Two hours. Where are we going?"

"I'm going after Mordred and the *Wilma Deering*," Rogers said. "You're staying here."

"I volunteer, sir!"

"I'd use you if I could," Rogers said. "And you know why I can't. Now listen to what I want you to do."

Mordred continued with more bombast than bombing; though he claimed to be destroying most of North America no further nuclear fires had been lit.

"I think he's having more trouble than he lets on," Major Dupre said as Rogers slipped behind his desk.

"See if we can get in touch with him," Rogers said, "And get communications to patch in every gang that's willing to listen."

"Prince Mordred, I don't know how many atomic bombs you've got up there," Rogers began, "But you haven't a week's worth of air or water. You can keep making those funny noises, or you can come down. And remember, *Sonny*, the longer you wait, the harder the licking."

"Enough bombs to wipe out your puny civilization!" the prince screamed.

Perhaps he was bluffing, but Rogers couldn't take chances. "Why have no more bombs fell? You have a problem—before you can solve it," Rogers said, "we will have revived the first thousand Prl'lu in the chambers at Mount Erebus."

Mordred halted. Rogers wished the scope was clearer. Had his pupils dilated?

"Do not use that weapon, dear Father," Mordred said. "My doing so was a mistake. For you it will be a disaster."

"I can deal with the Prl'lu."

"The Prl'lu do not deal with lesser breeds. I, hereditary leader of the Han, had difficulty. We used force to seize the death ray. Twenty five of my Man-Din were destroyed. The Prl'lu are our military, ancient and terrible, warehoused here while there were no wars to fight. They are warriors with powers beyond belief."

"We won," Rogers said.

"Against a mere handful! Their revivification machine malfunctioned, else we would all, even San-Li Mordred, be their slaves!"

"Their menace is gone," Rogers said. "Let us talk of the present."

"The Prl'lu are not confined to your one puny planet," Mordred said.

"The Prl'lu menace is suppressed," Rogers persisted. "You owe me—"

"I owe you for the destruction of the Empire of the Air Lords of Han! I owe you for the rape and degradation of my mother and my people. Yes, Father, there is much I owe you!"

Rogers suppressed the impulse to defend himself. The whole world tuned in and he had to get into this . . . but Rogers was in no position to spurn a weapon because its handle was dirty. "Perhaps I'm not so guilty as you presume," he began, but Mordred cut in.

"Guilty!" the Han prince cried. "Weighed and found wanting. It is finished!"

"Let me meet with you. Neither of us wants all Earth destroyed." I wish I believed that, Rogers thought.

"Why should I bargain with a bankrupt?" Mordred asked. "What can you offer?"

"The Prl'lu base in Antarctica, peace between Han and human."

"Peace with you heading the wild people as you did in my grandfather's day?"

"I will be your hostage," Rogers said.

Mordred bent nearer the lens and his face loomed. "Place yourself in my hands for trial and punishment."

"Agreed," Rogers said. "I'll come up in a small scout ship—one you can easily shoot down if you distrust me."

"Come," Mordred said. He turned and there was a momentary glimpse of Lu-An.

"No, Tony!" she shrieked. "He's sworn to kill you!" Someone grabbed her. Mordred reappeared. He said nothing.

"That female has been of consequence," Mordred said, "but her usefulness is—almost at an end. Betray me now, Rogers, and earth will see her flayed alive."

"I'm coming, Mordred," Rogers said.

"Tony," Ruth whispered, "Believe the Han woman. This is a trap."

"You're quite right," Rogers said cheerfully, "It is a trap. Come see me off."

Holcomb had forced the ship down within feet of the ground where it swayed, restrained by a thin ultron line.

"What's that thing on the side of the ship?" Ruth Harris asked.

"Excalibur," Rogers said. He kissed her and squeezed into the partly open canopy.

"Tools and oxygen in the back seat," Holcomb said, "and a back pack frame you can use as a belt. Good luck and godspeed, sir!"

Rogers saluted and closed the canopy. "Ordinance," he called, "have you takeoff data for me?"

The tech gave him the numbers. Rogers swung the ship around and up, checked his heading, and turned on the *dis* jets. The weightless *Eagle* rose rapidly. He held his speed, climbing until the sky turned black. He shut off the now useless *dis* jets, and adjusted the ultrascope. The *Wilma Deering* came advancing over the western rim of the world. "And now," he grunted, "we see who shoots first."

The ships approached each other through the void. Using the last of his maneuvering gas, Rogers got the *Eagle* turned so the ship and its attached weapon faced the larger *Wilma*. The range shortened. The minutes of his life ticked off.

Ground contact assured him he was on a collision orbit with the *Wilma Deering*. So what else was new? The remnants of the military council watched his relayed ultraprobe signal as the big space ship swung nearer. To Rogers' eyes she was only another bright speck in the sky, moving slightly against the turning background of the constellations. Still out of range. He adjusted his probe. Ruth had been right! Parts of the intertron shielding had either been removed or not yet installed. Amid the dull sheen of inertron on the *Wilma's* underside were huge gleaming patches of steel.

Only ten kilometers away! The death ray killed rats at two kilometers.

His vidplate brightened and Mordred's face appeared. "Just in case you thought to surprise the Prince of the Imperial Han," he greeted. The screen widened. Lu-An stood proud and erect between redcoated guards. She was laced into a strait-jacket of black leather. Arms bound, she waited. The black restraint covered her slender body from neck to hips. Her long legs and bare feet were free.

"She will be near the airlock where any explosion will destroy her first," Mordred said conversationally. "When you come within range you will abandon your ship which will then be destroyed. You will jump to the hatch which will be open and lighted to receive you." He turned as someone spoke out of range of the transmitter.

Rogers fussed with the probe scope. He picked up movement, refined his focus, saw two guards leading Lu-An. Her face was obscured but she tossed black hair in a defiant gesture.

Brave girl, Han fanatics, insane son. Balanced against how many human lives? Young Holcomb,

Ruth Harris, old Entallador and his lovely daughter . . . Rogers' hand cupped over the switch.

"Marshal Rogers," Mordred's voice brought him out of his reverie. "What have you attached to the side of your ship?"

"You took our only spaceship." Rogers hoped he sounded casual. Range three kilometers. "My technicians jury rigged air tanks to the dis jet. As you can see, it was damaged during takeoff." Range two point seven.

Mordred spoke in rapid Han to the man at the scanner. "Karnak ray? Stand aside. Let me look!" He swore, turned back to the screen where he saw Rogers inside the Eagle, hands motionless. "Kill him!" Mordred screamed. "Kill him now!"

Aboard the Eagle a red light flashed. Rogers slumped face down, hands still spread over the console. On the Wilma Deering Mordred bolted from his chair. "Cheated. Cheated! I wanted him alive!"

Three hundred kilometers below, so did Ruth Harris want him alive. Holcomb took her arm. On the rangefinder beneath Rogers' inert hand the clicking numbers read two-point-one-six.

Mordred's staff shrank from his rage as he kicked subordinates and lifeless instruments. Finally he was still.

Finally a Han lieutenant dared speak. "Lord, what do we with the ship? It still approaches." The ultrabeam communicator in front of the captain's chair was still on. The empty chair filled the screens at Niagra and aboard the Eagle. Faint Han voices were heard as Mordred responded, "Blast him with rep rays. Knock him into space. Emptiness is a fitting tomb for the enemies of Han."

Range one point nine zero.

Rogers moved his right hand. The ultraphone went silent. He kept the death ray on, unsure of its spread or the orientation of his ship. "Niagra?" he called.

"Here, Marshal."

"Drs. Tanaka and Wolsky's treatment worked again. I didn't need the cardiac stimulator." He opened his armored vest and plucked metal discs from his skin. The *Wilma Deering* loomed close. The orbits were not exact; He would have to cross nearly a hundred meters of empty space. He turned off the death ray—less than a minute after he first turned it on. "Going outside," he said, and latched his helmet.

He opened the ultron shield. Air whooshed and the tanks behind him floated toward the airless void. Rogers grabbed them, attached his air hose to one, and turned a valve. The other, fitted with controls like a flying belt, he slipped onto his back. He snapped the tool kit to his belt. Uncoiling the ultron mooring line, he kicked off for the space ship "overhead."

Fifty years of weightless flying made it easy. The air tank was a crude substitute for a *dis* powered belt but here there was no air. The main difference, he thought, was the confusing lack of a *down* in his inner ear. For a man less accustomed to the violent motions of belting, it could easily have turned into nausea.

There was a handhold beside the airlock. He snapped the ultron mooring line onto it. As he tried the lock the line pulled taut and the *Eagle* stopped drifting.

The airlock would not open. Hand over

gauntleted hand, Rogers worked his way down the hull to the gleaming bare steel where inertron had been removed. He fished in his tools for a magnetic anchor and used it to brace himself while dissing a hole in the hull. Moist air exploded outward, enveloping Rogers in a shimmering cloud of ice crystals. It had been nearly three minutes since he had rayed the ship.

With desperate haste he wrenched the circular piece of hull outward and hurled himself into the ship, dis ray at ready. The empty compartment was crew's quarters. The door had closed when pressure dropped. Rogers pulled the disc back into position, jammed it with a pair of toggle bolts and covered the gap with a plastic patch. Then he advanced on the door. He shed his air tanks and drew weapons. Pressure equalized and the door opened. Two dead Han floated in the corridor. Rogers arrowed for the control room.

When commissioned the *Wilma Deering* was to have carried a one man scout in a lower compartment. Its intended place was filled by a Prl'lu craft, sleek and black.

Dead Han filled the forward compartments. In the control room bodies were everywhere. Mordred drifted face down under the captain's chair. It was over five minutes since Rogers had keyed the death ray. The probability of reviving anyone was dropping logarithmically. The once powerful Han were wiped out. Rogers put the death ray in his belt and pulled out the heart stimulator. Lights on the communicator flashed. He kept searching.

Lu-An was in an aft cabin, floating between the corpses of her guards. When he caught her in his arms she opened her eyes. "Tony. Am I still to live then?"

"Lu-An, my God, you're breathing!"

"That is a hopeful sign," she said as she struggled with the strait jacket. Impulsively Rogers kissed her before he cut her loose. Fortunately he had freed her of her leather imprisonment before he learned that beneath it she was naked. "Mordred put this on me," she said, and showed him a metal disc glued below her left breast. "He said it would protect me."

The light dawned.

"Mordred!" Rogers flew out the hatch, weapons ready. He searched the control room. Mordred's "body" was gone. "Lu-An," he shouted, "Stay where you are while I search the ship." *Dis* gun drawn, Rogers searched the *Wilma Deering* again. When he saw the Prl'lu scout ship was gone he stopped.

Then he went back through the ship and examined the *bona fide* corpses. They were all dead; he chucked them through the airlock. By this time Lu-An was in the captain's seat, talking with Holcomb on the ultrabeam. "Here he is," she said, and turned to Rogers.

"Hi, Tony," Holcomb grinned.

"I'm fine," Rogers said. "But Mordred gave me the slip."

"Looks like you've got the situation well . . . in hand," Holcomb said. "And I'll bet that's the best look humans have ever had at a Han princess."

My God, and aboard Wilma! "Lu-An, hurry up and get some clothes on!" Later during the hours of descent after he had cast off the *Eagle* for later retrieval he could ask, "What happened to you?"

"Mordred sent me out of the control room. I thought he was going to kill me. I didn't care. When I came to you were holding me."

"Ah well, things are pretty well under control now."

"Yes, my love."

"On the other hand," he said, thinking of Ruth, "I think our troubles may have just begun."

Later, he would have time to think about his son.

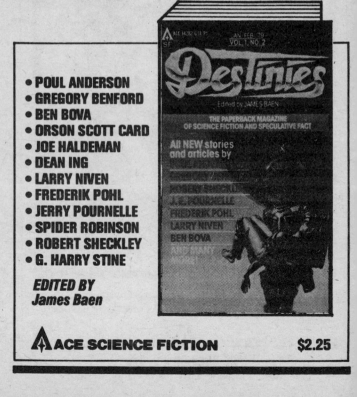